HEALTHY
THINKING

HEALTHY THINKING

HOW TO TURN LIFE'S LEMONS INTO LEMONADE

TV'S 'ATTITUDE DOCTOR'
DR TOM MULHOLLAND

Healthy Thinking™, Emotional Algebra™ and The Attitude Doctor™ are trademarks of Dr Tom Mulholland

First published in India in 2006
by arrangement with Reed Publishing (NZ) Ltd, New Zealand.
Reprinted June, July 2006

ISBN 81-8328-036-6

Published by
Wisdom Tree
4779/23 Ansari Road
Darya Ganj
New Delhi-110002
Ph.: 23247966/67/68

Printed at
Print Perfect
C-209/1 Mayapuri II
New Delhi-110064

This book is dedicated to Dr Mike Cox,
friend, pilot and adventurer,
who took his own life after years
of battling his thoughts

Disclaimer

The ideas offered in this book are entirely the opinions of the author, a registered medical practitioner, and in no way represent case-by-case advice. As such, neither the author nor the publishers accept any responsibility for the personal actions of any reader, or for the outcomes produced by them, based on anything they read in this book. In cases of depression, it remains our view that you should always consult a medical practitioner.

Acknowledgements

My sincere thanks to:

My children — Olivia, Thomas, Sammie and Auburne — for teaching me many things and coming on many, many adventures.

Dr William Peters for being such a good friend.

Graeme Beals of Zenith Publishing Group for making the book possible and his editorial input.

My family for giving me the opportunity to achieve my goals.

Patients, colleagues and clients, who have taught me humility and humour, and enabled me to be part of their lives.

Warwick Grey and the teams at Microsoft, Hewlett Packard, Telecom and the Chamber of Commerce for their support.

To all these people and everyone else, thanks. I couldn't have done it without you and had so much fun at the same time.

Contents

Foreword

Over the years, as a professor of psychiatry, I have seen many people struggle with their thoughts and emotions. Doctors face the same life stressors and challenges as anyone else plus a few others that can influence their mental health and performance.

I know Dr Tom Mulholland as a friend and professional colleague. He is an enthusiastic, successful and intelligent doctor and entrepreneur — one of those people who has real flair and charisma, and who is never forgotten.

Tom has written an inspirational book. It is a very readable guide to how to think in a healthy way. He draws on his own experience of the highs and lows of business and personal life and how to turn an average day into a great day.

This book will be a useful guide for those who are successful but need a tune up as well as for those who are struggling and need some guidance. It will provide motivation and inspiration in dealing with everyday activities. It will help you cope with the big challenges that life can throw at you. It has the power to teach you how to be happy and to put you on the road to success.

I commend *Healthy Thinking* to you.

Professor Peter Yellowlees
Australia

Introduction

In seeking a title for this book I did a publications database search. The woman who searched for me said there were 3000 books with the word 'healthy' and 2000 with the word 'thinking' in the title but none called 'healthy thinking'.

'You are an original!' she said. People had been telling me that for years.

After 15 years of seeing patients and teaching them about healthy eating, healthy lifestyles and healthy exercise the key thing missing was healthy thinking. From my own personal experience I had discovered that unhealthy thinking causes unhealthy emotions and unhealthy attitudes, which can cause unhealthy behaviour. The same applied to my patients.

I have developed and taught the Healthy Thinking technique with amazing results. I have been practising healthy thinking for a number of years and thought it was time to write a book. I'm sure it will change your life as it has changed mine.

Healthy Thinking is like brain surgery without the blood. The more you practise it, the better you get. It's free, has no side effects and you don't need any medications or equipment. All you need are your thoughts and the tools I call Emotional Algebra.

You can change your attitude to suit and eliminate what I call the ten unhealthy emotions. These are stress, anger, anxiety, guilt, jealousy, resentment, rejection, sadness, frustration and disappointment. They are a waste of time and energy, and don't get you any further ahead.

I hope you learn the skills outlined in this book, and use them to become happy and enjoy the great life you can have. It's up to you. You can't change anyone else except yourself, though you will be surprised how people around you will change with your new attitudes.

This book is not intended to be an in-depth psychological or pharmacological textbook. There are plenty of those already. I hope it is an easy-to-read, how-to book on healthy thinking using my personal experiences as a doctor, entrepreneur, comedian and patient.

Of all the things I have done in my life the ability to think in a healthy way is the most powerful. Healthy Thinking will enable you to reach your goals and to live your dreams; not dream of the life you wish for but never create.

Dr Tom Mulholland
The Attitude Doctor

Part one

My journey to Healthy Thinking

Chapter 1

Misery

It was the first light I'd seen at the end of the tunnel that wasn't a train. I had found that my thinking was causing my misery. I had decided that I was allergic to being miserable. I was thinking in an unhealthy way.

This is not some flippant comment made for effect, but a conscious decision I made to avoid feeling awful.

I hated being miserable so much that I sought a cure, much like a rabid dog seeks water. That was once I got over the paralysis stage.

Like having your neck broken, being miserable can paralyse you. Fortunately, misery is a lot easier to cure, once you know how. My search for a cure for misery led me to discover the technique of Healthy Thinking.

Being miserable, unhappy, stressed or depressed is a serious business. It can kill you and has killed some of my friends, colleagues and patients as well as millions of people I have never met. So I think it is perfectly reasonable and protective to develop an allergy to such a condition.

Being miserable is not only unpleasant, it is a complete waste of time. You can feel sorry for yourself, but that won't cure misery. Normally it just feeds it.

There are many treatments for misery. Some work and some don't. I know because I tried most of them. I tried counselling, anti-depressants, alcohol and even overseas travel. I took almost everything except datura, because I never found anyone that had taken it twice. Anti-depressants helped but weren't a total answer. Some of the counselling was useful. Most of it wasn't. So I set off on a mission to find my own cure.

Until misery struck I had been a high achiever. I had gained a first-class honours degree in molecular biology, a medical degree, a pilot's licence, a sports medicine diploma, founded successful start-up companies and won business awards. I had been a forest ranger, survived a tidal wave while surfing in Java, and had doctored for the Fijian rugby team. I had travelled extensively and was an adrenalin junkie having leapt out of planes, climbed in New Zealand's Southern Alps, been in the Himalayas, flown through a hurricane (Hugo) to Central America, trekked through jungles, slept by a lagoon of crocodiles, dived with sharks in Tahiti, surfed huge waves and enough other exploits as to make Indiana Jones look very sedate.

So what was making me so miserable? After all I had just raised millions of dollars of venture capital for www.doctorglobal.com. I had founded this company and spent a lot of hard work and money (my own and that of friends and family) in doing so. I had a beautiful family with young children, a lovely country house a few minutes' drive from some of the world's best surf, plus all the toys I could want (well, nearly).

The reason I was feeling miserable was that my wife had just told me she was leaving. Not leaving to buy me a present or to do the shopping but leaving the marriage, as in she didn't want to be my wife any more.

My family, my dream was shattered, broken like a plate glass window on a cold winter's day. I could write a million books on how that felt but like all allergies it's best to avoid the trigger and move on. The voyage of discovery seeking a cure for my allergy to misery took me six months.

As a doctor and scientist, I had done original academic research on suicide, reminiscence in the elderly and other scientific projects, which had gained recognition and awards. I was an explorer in the physical and academic sense. But like the Holy Grail there was always something missing. It took this major setback in my life to send me to the heart of darkness, the temple of doom, to seek and find the answer.

The answer is such a simple discovery but it is the most powerful discovery I have ever made. It is so powerful I believe it could change the world, even prevent wars. It can certainly make you happy. I called my discovery Healthy Thinking.

I had used Healthy Thinking before, unknowingly, to treat my anxiety while surfing. That anxiety had been triggered when I was hit by a 20-foot tidal wave, but more of that in the next chapter.

Chapter 2

The first tidal wave

I love surfing waves. Surfing is my favourite sport. I spent many years at university chasing waves and travelled the planet surfing. Surfing has changed my life. I live where I do because it is close to some of the most consistent waves in the world.

I was recently featured in a book, *New Zealand Surfers: 25 Profiles of Kiwis Who Love to Surf* by Luke Williamson. In it, Luke wrote:

> Tom is an adventurer in the business, intellectual and surfing sense. A man who sets himself lofty goals and invariably exceeds them, Tom knows no boundaries. He is determined to have a good and exciting life that incorporates his dreams, his family and lots of surfing.

Anxiety, however, nearly made me stop surfing. At one stage surfing was a nightmare, rather than a dream.

In 1995 I had returned to Grajagan, East Java, in Indonesia as the camp doctor. G-Land, as it is known in surfing legend, has a famous left-hand wave that peels across a sharp reef and can become life-threatening when the swells are large. It is very remote and sits on the edge of the Javanese jungle, which is inhabited by scorpions, tigers, poisonous snakes and malaria. Soon, I was to find out exactly how life-threatening a place it could be.

Doctors would go to G-Land for free, treating the everyday casualties, from those who have nearly drowned to those who have been scraped across the reef. One day I sutured seven surfers. The benefit was still far bigger than the risk though. Grajagan is a wonderful place and, like Pipeline or Tavarua, is a world-class wave.

Puma, the camp manager, welcomed me back for my second year of duty. 'Doctor Tom,' he said, 'you can have Gerry Lopez's hut, right on the water's edge.'

In two days that hut would catch the full brunt of a 20-foot-high tsunami (tidal wave) triggered by an earthquake in the Java Trench. It would kill about 350 people in the Grajagan bay and villages, and injure many more.

On my first introduction to the huge surf the previous year, I had got a lift from two Hawaiians in an inflatable boat out to the back of the large 12- to 15-foot surf. At the time I had a chest infection and was riding a small board (7 foot 2 inches) in comparison to the 9-foot guns the Waimea Bay veterans were riding. I was unprepared and under-gunned for the mountains of water that were moving faster than trucks and exploding on the sharp and shallow reef. I was way out of my depth.

Out of breath I paddled up these huge faces — as big as three-storey buildings — as white plumes like rooster tails streamed off the crests. It was survival out there and I began to panic. After four hours and catching just one wave, I made it to shore, relieved to be on terra firma and alive.

A year later with that big-wave fear in my thoughts I settled into bed in the thatch hut about 20 feet from the high-tide mark. I knew my limitations as a surfer now, and was fitter and better prepared than the previous year. I felt I was ready to tame the Grajagan monster. I had a bigger board and a clear chest, and I excitedly anticipated the morning and the waves it would bring. They came sooner than I thought.

During the evening, several pro surfers, including Simon Law, Bob Bain, Shane Herring and Ritchie Lovett, who had arrived in the camp that day, had talked of a huge swell that was approaching from Western Australia. It sounded exciting.

It was 35°C at midnight when I climbed under my mosquito net. At 2 a.m. I was woken by the roar of large surf, a sound I had heard many times before, but this was louder. Initially I thought the big swell had arrived. But something was different. Normally when a wave breaks on a reef the initial explosion is separated by a lesser noise until the next wave cracks like a gun. This time the noise was getting louder and louder with no respite. I thought it must be a tropical rainstorm, then a jumbo jet off course from Jakarta.

It sounded low and as if it was going to crash. Instinctively I reached for my medical bag, expecting casualties as the jet crashed. The noise was so loud now that I thought the plane was going to crash on me. It is the loudest noise I have ever heard. I have stood on the runway when a 747 jet takes off and it was louder than that. When I felt the ground shake beneath me, I knew it wasn't a plane.

I felt a huge presence like a monster about to engulf me. I looked up through the door and in the gloom saw a 20-foot-high, brown, churning, foaming ocean charging towards me like a dam had burst. I knew it was a tidal wave. It certainly wasn't Father Christmas.

In the first second I felt sick, and an intense sadness as I thought that this was the end. My wife was pregnant with our first child, Olivia.

Not the big sleep now, I thought. I wasn't ready. I still had too much to do. Looking back, I believe I was not scared, as I thought I would die — there seemed no alternative.

In the next second I screamed '... it's a tidal wave!' and woke my friend Dr David Arden, a sound sleeper, who was also in the hut. The adrenalin hit, and in a reflex action I smashed through the back of the hut, still naked and still under my mosquito net.

In the third second the charging ocean engulfed me. In the dark I was tumbled and tossed like I was of little consequence. I heard the snapping of trees and thumps as large chunks of coral hit the ground. I was carried for what seemed like an age into the jungle, waiting for the white light at the end of the tunnel. But it never came.

My knees and hands hit the ground and momentarily I was released from the force of the sea. Then I heard a huge sucking noise as the sea retreated from the jungle. Now I was scared.

The thought that I would be dragged back into the bay and over the coral generated real fear. I realised that, if I could hold on, I might live. I had a chance. I hung on to the roots and trees for my very life. The water receded without me in its grip.

When I thought I was certain to die I felt no fear, as there was nothing I could do to save myself from what was to come. However, when I thought I would be sucked out to sea, I felt fear. Knowing I just had to survive the wave withdrawing, I knew I could do something to save myself. I knew that if I could hold on I might avoid dying or being severely injured on the razor-sharp reef. The thought created the feeling.

The feeling of fear and anxiety made me hold on for my life. Anxiety and fear have evolved to protect us from harm. This was just the sort of situation in which such emotions are useful. It is when thoughts create feelings that are irrational that they become unhealthy, as I will show in later chapters.

The sound of the ocean retreating was replaced by human screams. In the dim light, with my pupils wide, I saw a white surfboard. It had been swept through the jungle beside me. I grabbed it and put the leg rope around my ankle and charged through the jungle and up a small hill to where the unaffected part of the camp was awakening. There I was: naked, scratched, cut and scared … but alive!

Once I had secured a pair of shorts I began to assess the damage and to treat the casualties. Unfortunately some of the native shell collectors who slept on the water's edge had been badly hit. I noticed a native woman, silent, though her upper arm was bent at 90°, a fracture of the humerus. I did my best to straighten the woman's arm, gave her some medication, put her in a sling and watched as she disappeared into the night to check the fate of her family in the neighbouring village.

One surfer had smashed ribs, a badly cut face and a probable partially collapsed lung. I debated whether to insert the chest drain I had carried with me to let the blood and air out. A chest drain is like a large metal skewer with a plastic sheath. You insert the metal spike being careful not to hit any important structures like the heart or aorta. You then remove the metal part to leave a plastic drain in place. This would be no easy task in the gloom, illuminated only by fading torchlight.

I opted for conservative management and didn't use the drain. Slowly he got better and lived to leave the jungle in the next couple of days.

The carnage that was the aftermath is best told elsewhere but the smell, the chaos and the strong emotions I will never forget. The next day the jungle was full of strange sea creatures and the bay was full of sharks. Media accounts claimed more than 350 people died that night in the surrounding villages, mostly fishermen and children swept into the bay. I spent a few anxious days as we felt aftershocks, and slept on higher ground, fearing another tsunami.

I left G-Land three days later on the first boat that could get in. My family had experienced three anxious days not knowing if I was dead or alive. If the tide had been high at the time or the tsunami had arrived during the day while we were surfing more people would have died, perhaps including me. As it was, nature flicked me with its tail and I lived to surf another day, but that certainly wasn't the end of the experience.

Afterwards, I began to notice an anxiety while surfing. The trigger was the sight or sound of any large wave breaking. My throat would go dry and all I wanted to do was to get out of the water. Slowly but surely, smaller waves triggered the anxiety until waves only head high would generate an overwhelming desire to get out of the water. Surfing was my life. I loved the fitness, the feeling of sitting in the ocean and the thrill of riding a wave. It got to the point, however, that I was too scared to paddle out.

Normally I would paddle out on big days for the thrill. Now, in waves that were safe I was experiencing an irrational fear of being held down. It was starting to ruin my sport. I was developing avoidance strategies like back pain or fake injuries once the surf was huge. Even when the surf was small I felt scared.

I began to realise that the trigger for my anxiety was seeing a large set of waves approaching in the distance.

Ninety percent of the time those waves never broke on my head or held me down. I either could paddle out of the way or they broke far out to sea or away from me. I began to focus on the wave in front of me as I was paddling out. I was being anxious over 90 percent of waves that wouldn't affect me.

I now know that around 90 percent of things that people worry about or get anxious over never happen. Getting stressed or anxious may even make them more likely to happen. In my case I was more likely to get hurt owing to lack of confidence. When you paddle for a wave you must be committed and get to your feet early. To delay or try and avoid the drop may cause you to wipe out and become injured. Even worse, anxiety causes your heart to race, which uses up precious oxygen under the water. My unhealthy thinking was creating an irrational anxiety that was stopping me doing the sport I enjoy the most — surfing. I had to act.

I began to examine my thoughts. I forced myself to get fit, to hold my breath for 30 seconds and to count every time I was held under a wave. I found I was never held under for more than 10 seconds. The more I panicked underwater and thrashed for the surface, the less I could hold my breath. I changed my thought to, 'I can hold my breath for long enough'. I began to relax underwater and consume less oxygen. I began to take on bigger surf and stopped using avoidance strategies like back pain.

Once again, I began to enjoy the feeling of being hit by a wave, being tumbled around as if in a washing machine and popping up the back like a cork: well, maybe a waterlogged one! It took a lot of courage to overcome my anxiety by controlling my thoughts, but I got out there and my life is the better for it. Instead of worrying about the waves that wouldn't hit me, I concentrated only on the one in front of me. This helped and I began to take on bigger and bigger surf. Now, I stay fit, am surfing better than ever, and am once again comfortable in the water and enjoying something I almost gave up.

You may be thinking that being hit by a tidal wave is an unusual event and that you too would have been scared to go back into the water. The point is that the tsunami triggered unhealthy thinking. Most of us don't need a 20-foot-high wall of water to create anxiety or unhealthy thinking.

Take a moment to consider some of the things that cause you anxiety. Now think of them as a set of waves in terms of the distance they are from you. Some will be far away; some will be closer. Now consider that the more distant waves may never hit you. You are more likely to be harmed by something right in front of you than something far away so concentrate on the closest, most pressing ones. Think them through more clearly and in a more healthy way.

With regard to my fear of the surf, by identifying the trigger (the waves in the distance) and changing my thought (it won't hit me and I can hold my breath), I changed my negative emotional reaction to a healthy one (from anxiety to enjoyment).

Anxiety is a major cause of illness and unhappiness. In its extreme form it paralyses people to the point that they can't leave home or do the things they love the most. In its mildest form it can make people avoid taking risks or just inhibit their growth. Over the years I have always been uncomfortable prescribing anxiolytics such as Valium for anxiety as I believe it masks the problem. Anti-depressants such as Paroxetine can be more effective by increasing serotonin levels in the brain. I believe that Healthy Thinking is also effective and have used it with good effect on myself, and patients, either with or without medication.

I am a pilot with hundreds of hours of flying experience. I have thousands of hours of experience as a passenger. I love flying. If every time I took off I thought that the plane might crash, I would feel anxious and never fly. If I thought that the plane would never crash I wouldn t do my safety checks and so create greater risk for others and myself. Again, the point is that what I am thinking controls my emotions, which in turn can influence my behaviour.

Remember that 90 percent of what you worry about, like waves in the distance, may never affect you.

Focus on the task in hand and you are more likely to prevent what you fear most from ever happening.

Chapter 3

Live your dream, don't dream your life

The best way, I believe, to achieve your goals is to combine Healthy Thinking with Success Behaviours.

Someone said to me recently that what impressed them about me is that I actually do what I say I'm going to do. Man does what man says! Most people talk about things they want to do or good ideas they have but never actually do anything about bringing them about. I do.

It is interesting the reaction I have had over the years to my ideas and how that reaction changes each time I bring a dream to life and live it. One of my first dreams was to be a doctor. I remember being on a large ship a few years ago and running into someone who knew me when I was five years old. She said, 'You are the only person I know who at five years old said he was going to be a doctor and a brain surgeon and did it.' I guess I am a brain surgeon without the blood, teaching people to operate on their own thoughts.

In fact, no one in my family had ever been to university

before. Many people assume that my father is a doctor. I get it all the time. But my father and grandfathers had either been to sea or worked on the wharves. It was likely I would go to sea, which I nearly did, and yet for some reason I battled to become a doctor instead. That story shows my determination and the early stages of development of Healthy Thinking.

At school I did okay but wasn't the hardest working student. I knew that I loved the forest and used to earn money by trapping opossums and selling skins. I decided that I wanted to join the New Zealand Forest Service as a forest ranger trainee. I didn't think I had the academic marks to be a doctor. As luck would have it, I applied to the Forest Service from school and, in 1979 at age 17, was one of the 30 successful forest ranger trainees from the 800 applicants from across the country.

I left home on a bus with all my worldly goods to start my education. I arrived at a forestry town called Turangi to begin a year of labouring in Lake Taupo forest.

I remember being the only white guy, the only one without a tattoo and the only one without a criminal record in a pruning gang. Each day we'd pull into the local prison and pick up what were affectionately known as boobheads — inmates. It amazed me at the time how a whole prison could be full of people convicted for unpaid parking fines.

My naivety was shattered when I asked another prisoner what he was in for. 'Murder,' came the reply.

Always wanting to push the boundaries I asked in my politest voice, 'Why did you murder someone?'

'For asking too many stupid bloody questions,' he said.

So I did a year of fighting fires, using chainsaws, rescuing lost people and jumping out of helicopters. My goal was to keep my mouth shut before someone shut it for me.

At the end of the year I was bright-eyed, bushy-tailed and off to university to do a forestry degree. I was employed by the government and did two years of study, working all my holidays in the mountains, shooting deer and identifying plants. I'd be dropped off by helicopter in a remote region for eight weeks with one or two other rangers and we'd survive on dehydrated food, the deer we shot and the trout we caught. We would come out for a week at Christmas and then go in for another eight weeks. I loved it.

I was fit and healthy and there was a sense of satisfaction that at the end of four months I could look and know that I had crossed every river and sat on every mountaintop.

After a while, however, I yearned for something more intellectual and I still had the desire to help people. I still wondered whether I could be a doctor.

So one day I hitchhiked four hours to the University of Otago Medical School in Dunedin, having arranged a meeting with the associate dean. She informed me that if I pulled out of forestry school, completed a BSc in botany with two As and two Bs I would get into medical school. This meant I had to pay back my salary to the government, change courses and do another year of study.

I hitchhiked back to Christchurch, met the Forest Service and my father and resigned my position. My bosses in the Forest Service laughed and said I would never get into medical school. My father didn't laugh. He told me that I was a complete idiot throwing away a good job and that I would never get into medical school because I wasn't up to it.

Full of self-confidence and determined to prove them wrong, I enrolled in botany, paid the money and studied hard, eventually exceeding the dean's requirements with two As and two B pluses.

Happy with my performance I headed north for the summer break and ran a guided walks programme in a forest park. That is, I got a book out of the library and learnt a few stars then organised a night walk. Despite it being cloudy with no stars in sight, 200 people turned up. I wasn't sure if I had a really good idea or whether everyone was just bored and looking for something to do. As the cloud cover persisted, I eventually drew the stars on a blackboard and took the crowd walking in the dark to see glow-worms.

I used to take groups into a cave we had found. When I turned off the torch, the glow-worms would shine like the stars. The next best thing. Everyone sighed in delight but one child went 'Ooogh!' I then warned them not to scream. I turned the torch to the roof to reveal several hundred large cave wetas (large scary insects). I said not to scream or the wetas might fall on their heads. The child sighed with delight while everyone else went 'Ooogh!' I'm not sure if it was Healthy Thinking on the child's part, but the reaction was certainly different.

That was one of the best jobs I ever had. I felt like David Bellamy, showing adults and children the plants, animals and ecosystems of the forest.

Then two letters arrived at my little camp in the forest. One was from the University of Otago Medical School, the oldest and some argue the most prestigious in the country. With trepidation, I opened the envelope.

> Dear Mr Mulholland,
> Due to the intense nature of competition and the unusually high standard of applicants this year, you have been unsuccessful in gaining entry to the University of Otago Medical School.

The second letter was from a girl I was madly in love with, or so I thought.

> Dear Tom,
> I thought I had better let you know that I will be shifting to another city as I have just got engaged to someone called Guy. He has just been accepted into medical school and we are going to live together.

Perhaps I was lucky there wasn't a third letter.

The arrival of those two letters was a defining moment. It didn't worry me that everyone had told me I would never get into medical school and I hadn't. I wanted to be a doctor and now I couldn't. As for the girl, well ... never mind. I hadn't met the best woman in the world yet.

I walked for an hour into the forest and sat by a deep pool looking at my reflection. I threw stones and watched the rings get bigger and bigger. I felt like going to London. I would leave the country and pursue my interest in punk rock music by joining a band. I had it all planned. I would work as a bouncer, a barman ... and probably clean toilets, as I had done to pay my way through university.

Have a degree in botany but work as a bouncer?, I eventually thought. Same s**t, different city! I didn't mind doing it but didn't want to do it for the rest of my life.

I thought some more. I had enjoyed the paper on genetics and molecular biology. Despite not being in the honours programme, I decided to ring the university the next day (some 1000 miles from my forest camp). I wanted to see if they would accept me as an honours student, which meant another year of university study. I thought and believed I could still get into medical school. So I constructed a plan.

I remember talking to the Dean of Zoology and was grateful I hadn't called him a few names for the way he had treated some students that year. Beware the toes you stand on today because they may be connected to the ass you have to kiss tomorrow! So I kissed plenty of ass and was accepted as an honours student in zoology majoring in molecular biology and genetics.

I suffered the jibes of, 'I told you that you wouldn't get into medical school,' but focusing on my goal, I worked my butt off.

My grandfather thought it was great as now doing zoology I could get a job in a zoo! I could!

One day I'll write another book on how hard I worked that year. I worked till 4 a.m. in the lab, radioactively labelling DNA and looking for cellular messengers. I worked as a waiter and a barman to pay my tuition fees.

One day I was serving a group of people and had a tray of champagne. Most people were taking the champagne without looking at the waiter, as is custom. They were too busy talking to their important colleagues. However, unlike everyone else, one man turned, looked me right in the eye and said, 'Thank you very much.' It was the then Governor-General of New Zealand, Sir David Beattie.

I have never forgotten that lesson in charm and how influential it can be on another person. Perhaps the most important person in the country had looked me in the eye and made me feel important. This simple act had made another person feel successful and valued. It cost him only one second and a smile.

My hard work and commitment was later paid off with four A pluses, an A and a first-class honours degree. It didn't get any better. I got a letter from the University of Otago Medical School accepting me as a second-year medical student. I got a letter from the girl saying that she had broken up with Guy and asking what I was doing.

Some years later Guy phoned me up and asked if I wanted to flat with him in our new town as first-year doctors. We did, but that's another story.

I headed south with all my worldly goods. This time they fitted into a VW Beetle rather than a suitcase on a bus. I told my dad and the forest service that I was going to medical school and I told my granddad that I wasn't going to work in the zoo. I was anxious as I thought I would be inferior intellectually to the other students. Again, I was allowing negative thoughts to dictate how I felt.

My assigned lab partner was William Peters, who was to become my best friend and business partner. The professor of surgery asked us on our first day what school we went to. William had been dux of arguably the most prestigious school in the country, Kings College. I had been to a rough school called Taita College, which at the time could have resembled something from the Bronx in New York. I certainly didn't have an academic pedigree and I left to enhance my education elsewhere. I have heard that the school is much improved now.

I found that the way to seem smarter was to turn up five minutes before William, and then he was always asking me what was going on. That way he always knew less than me. After a while I realised he was no smarter than me and we could turn up at the same time. I got confidence in my academic ability. Medical school was easy after an honours degree and I passed every year with flying colours.

Over the years I have lived out and achieved many dreams in reality, but Healthy Thinking and Success

Behaviours have always been the key tools with which I have worked. I just did not recognise them at that time for what they were. Nor had I formally thought them through and refined them into a simple, transferable whole as I now have.

For example, while I was at medical school I needed money. My parents offered me some of their hard-earned money but I wanted to make my own way. William was a live-in tutor at Christ's College, another prestigious New Zealand School. I suggested we start a tutoring service for schoolchildren. We went to a small business tutorial and were advised to choose a business partner more carefully than we would choose a wife. We both looked at each other and laughed. We still do.

I nearly didn't start the tutoring school because of my thinking. I was worried that we would be pandering to the wealthy: they would be the only ones who could afford to pay for private tutoring. Their children would become better educated, further widening the gap between the rich and the poor and uneducated. I decided if business boomed we would offer free tuition to those whose parents couldn't afford it.

How wrong I was. The phone went for the first time. William and I, dressed in our $2 suits from the Salvation Army thrift shop, drove out to a working-class suburb called Linwood to meet our first client. We were to meet the parents of a girl called Heidi.

The house was attached to a corner store. We pulled up in our $300 car and walked through the shop into the house. We matched Heidi with our extensive database of tutors. We had only one at that stage, with William and myself as back-up.

Carol was a medical student and I would have paid money for her to tutor me. Luckily Carol and Heidi matched. I was amazed when Heidi's dad booked 20 lessons in advance, walked to the till and pulled out $300 in cash. We had just paid for the car. Mind you we still had to pay Carol. That was one of my first lessons in cash flow. Anyway I was excited that the concept had worked and that we weren't educating only the rich. To my knowledge, private tutoring schools didn't really exist in that format then.

The Christchurch Tutoring Service was a great success and each week medical students would stay behind after lectures to collect their pay from us. At one stage we had about 30 tutors working for us and business was booming. I gathered enough money, sold my VW and headed to Canada and the US for a skiing holiday. Three months later I returned to start my fifth year of medical school and we passed the business on to another medical student the following year, as William and I were too busy with another plan.

I had arrived in Christchurch to a phone call from William. He couldn't sell his car in Auckland so wanted to start a car fair when he returned to Christchurch. It was to be the first in the South Island. I liked the idea. People would pay $11 to drive their car into a parking lot for three hours on a Sunday. Buyers could enter free.

The city council gave us the car park on the condition that we donate a percentage of the take to a charity, to which we agreed. I approached the dean of our medical school, Professor Alan Clarke, for a suggestion of a worthy benefactor. The Canterbury Medical Research Foundation was the immediate response.

The car-parking superintendent insisted that we donate to something else as he thought what we were proposing was a scam. There followed a quick phone call from the dean to a public figure who was patron of the Canterbury Medical Research Foundation. Reassured that in fact the foundation funded groundbreaking medical research, the superintendent gave us the green light and we opened to a blizzard and 24 cars on our first day.

I phoned the local television station thinking they could use a good story. They filmed us and the next week 240 cars turned up!

After a while, a few car dealers turned up and threatened to run us out of town. They started a competing car fair in a residential suburb. They didn't do their homework and, interestingly, a phone call from an irate resident had them shut down. Just how the resident got irate remains a mystery and I'm not saying anything on the subject. It was a lot of fun and we funded our own way through medical school, plus provided a few more jobs.

William went on to be director of cardioscopic research at Stanford University in California. At age 26 he helped perform the first human heart bypass operation in the world using an endoscope. He used a device called an ascending aortic balloon catheter, or the endoclamp, a device that he had patented. This device became part of a company called Heartport, which did very well on the NASDAQ Stock Exchange.

I decided on a job and a lifestyle, and shifted to Taranaki, home of great surf. I tried my hand at training to be an orthopaedic surgeon. The long hours and always looking out at the surf while being stuck in the operating theatre frustrated me. I opted for a mix of working in the emergency department of the hospital and starting my own general and sports medicine clinic. After a time, I needed a new challenge.

I had always wanted to fly so decided to become a pilot. My dreams at night as a child were often of soaring over fields like a bird. Live your dreams, don't dream your life.

Once again an unhealthy thought almost stopped me. I saw an advertisement in the local newspaper for scholarships for learning to fly with the aero club. I said to a few friends that I was thinking of entering. 'They'll never give it to you. You are a doctor. Scholarships are for people that can't afford to fly,' came the response.

The problem is that if you listen to experts who have an opinion with no basis in fact, you will be like them: uninformed and no further ahead. With an hour to go before the closure deadline to pay the $120 to enter for the scholarship, I drove out to the airport and filled out the form. I remember thinking at the time that I will never win the scholarship by not entering. At least entering has to increase my chances.

As it turned out, I won a flying scholarship and am now a qualified pilot. I have flown helicopters, Cessnas and a Vampire jet, and had countless missions flying myself and friends to remote places surfing, skiing and fishing. In a Hong Kong simulator I have flown an Airbus after a bomb has exploded and I have tried to land a 747 with only one engine in an Auckland simulator while doing my aviation medicine diploma.

At school I had thought of applying to join the air force but another ill-informed amateur had told me that at 6 foot 3 inches I was too tall to be a pilot, as I would lose my knees should I have to eject. The thought of leaving my kneecaps in the plane while I ejected was too much, so safe in the knowledge I was too tall to be a pilot I chose another career. Why is it that sometimes when you tell people what you want to do they tell you all the reasons you can't do something?

If I had listened to all the reasons why I couldn't do the things I have done, I would still be in bed. From an early age I was told that I never had a musical bone in my body. Maybe I haven't, but I have played my guitar all over the world, have earned money busking in the streets, played in a band and even had crowds clap!

When I started the first private accident and emergency medical centre in my city I was told it would never survive. I was told I would be run out of town. People laughed at me, and doctors who had come to my wedding would cross the street, avoiding my eye.

I thought, You don't own patients. They will go where they get good service. As a doctor I am running a business, the business of keeping people healthy. What is good for the patient is good for the business!

That proved to be a very valuable business rule. Another one of my rules was don't let emotion get in the way of business. This was an early example of how I worked to keep unhealthy emotions out of business.

Against the odds, the occasional dirty tricks campaign and the fact that I was told most new businesses don't survive, I opened the walk-in clinic with X-ray, pharmacy, doctors and nurses and a 24-hour call system. I focused totally on patient care and providing a quality medical service.

Within a year the clinic had turned over $1,000,000 but, more importantly, had provided a much needed service and changed the way medicine was practised in the city. Now a host of other clinics have proliferated and patients have a choice of good medical care providing increased services in our community.

I decided to enter the clinic into the local Chamber of Commerce Business Awards. Once again the laughter came. (These days, I regard this as an indicator that I'm on track.) When people laugh at an idea I know that it is a new idea and I am about to explore new territory. Maybe I am an explorer but I like doing new things and exploring new niches. It makes for a wonderful, exciting and interesting life. It also provides more jobs.

A typical comment was:

> You can't enter a medical centre in the business awards. No one does it and it's not a business; it's a service.

Once again my attitude was that the clinic was a business and I wouldn't win if I didn't enter. So, full of enthusiasm, I filled out the entry forms at the last minute and eagerly awaited the judges' visit. Using the previous 'last-minute strategy', the visit was the next day. I answered all the questions. I then bought tickets to the finals ceremony. I was full of confidence, but as it turned out, unprepared for what lay ahead.

I had been asked to provide a logo so I thought our name would be in lights. I booked a large table for family and friends and dressed in my best and only suit. I told everyone we were finalists and we went to the awards. The finalists were read out and our name wasn't even mentioned. My table looked at me in disgust.

We clapped the finalists and winners. The night was a fizzer and I was disappointed. But what was I thinking? This didn't mean I didn't run a good clinic. It meant I hadn't prepared for the judges or the awards.

Maybe there were people there that were pleased I had failed, I don't know, but I certainly wasn't one of them. Rather than give up, I vowed to enter again next year, find out the rules and write a business plan. Experience is a wonderful thing.

Healthy Thinking and Success Behaviours had taught me that Michael Jordan never gave up if he didn't win the first basketball game of a season; Tiger Woods didn't stop playing golf if he missed a putt; Henry Ford didn't stop making cars when the first one didn't go.

The following year, not only was I prepared, my business was booming from writing a business plan and being focused. I was eating my meal when the MC announced that White Cross clinic was not only the winner of the best emerging business award, but had also been named the most innovative business, an award for which all businesses of all sizes entered that year were eligible. I received a plaque, a number of prizes and a letter from the chief executive:

> The 1997 Air New Zealand Taranaki Business Awards contained a number of innovative and highly successful business in varying stages of the business cycle. Foremost in the emerging business category was White Cross Taranaki, which went on to win. In their assessment the judges noted Tom Mulholland the Clinic Director has an impressive knowledge of the business and was very switched on and enthusiastic about its operation and operating environment. Also noted was that Tom Mulholland is to be commended for what has been achieved. He was the difference for White Cross Taranaki Ltd finishing first rather than second.

I was and still am proud of that letter. I didn't give up.

I believed in the vision of better health care and kept at it. We often try to instil the value of persistence in our children but I am amazed at how many adults don't adopt the same value in their own lives.

Five years after leaving White Cross I returned to help out the new owners, who are friends of mine. The first day back was really busy with many sick patients. I went home thinking I had had a bad day. That was a week ago. Tonight I have just got back from working my second shift. I used Healthy Thinking to change my day and make it fun for everyone. I chose my attitude, changed my thoughts and behaviour and had a great day.

I remembered to focus on each patient and to make each feel special. I saw sick children, looking scared, coming in on a cold night in their pyjamas. I asked one little boy with big eyes, 'Are you sick?'

'Yes,' he trembled.

'Well that's lucky, because I'm a doctor and I can make you all better again.'

I remembered what I felt like when I was sick and scared. I remembered how, when my children were sick, I made the decision to take them to the doctor. I thought of how it felt for me and for my children, and how a friendly face and smile helped us.

Rather than think of the many patients waiting and the fact that I hadn't had my dinner, I enjoyed the moment and the joy of seeing little kids smile. I didn't mind when a mother asked me to look in all her kids' ears because

I knew that when she got home, if one cried, she'd wish she'd had them all checked. I had a fun night.

Anyway back to the story. There will be more on how to do Healthy Thinking later.

The $5000 in prizes from the business awards enabled me to start another business. I couldn't find a dentist to occupy the vacant rooms in the clinic despite writing letters and personally visiting dentists to offer them rooms for only $100 per week with all the facilities needed for an emergency dental centre. So I rang a friend of mine whose brother was a dentist hundreds of miles away. I had offered it to all the locals first so felt no remorse in going further afield. We bought an old chair and I coined the phrase 'The gentle dentist, gentle on your mouth and gentle on your pocket'.

I used one of the prizes to pay for the freephone number 0800 TOOTHACHE. I found two good dentists from another city and convinced them to come to our province on a trial basis. The business flourished and we sold the business to the new dentists six months after taking the risk ourselves.

I remember having listened to Sir Tim Wallis, the father of deer recovery in New Zealand, an aviation pioneer, founder of Warbirds over Wanaka and The Helicopter Line. I had been to medical school with his niece and had met him again at an aviation medical conference.

He told me how he had bought one of the first

helicopters in the country. He had mortgaged his mother's house to do so. With something like 18 hours' flying experience he took off into the Southern Alps in front of a gathering nor'wester storm.

High in the mountains his crew had shot many deer and were about to strop them to the helicopter and fly them out. Tim leapt out of the helicopter into the snow to help tie the deer up as the storm was getting closer. The helicopter took off without him. He hadn't figured the weight differential. He told me he was more agile in those days and grabbed the skid of the unoccupied flying chopper. It came back to earth with a thud.

They took off and, to get enough airspeed, plunged over the edge with a number of deer strapped underneath. However the thud had produced a crack in the tail. The tail of the helicopter broke off and the machine crashed into a drift of snow. Fortunately everyone survived and walked out of the mountains.

The next day the bank manager turned up ready to call in the loan on Tim's mother's house.

'You can't do that,' he said. 'All this proves is that I'm not the pilot I thought I was. Lend me some more money and I will employ a real pilot. It doesn't mean deer recovery is a bad idea.'

The rest is now history. Tim became Sir Tim and deer recovery became a major New Zealand industry. That story motivated me many times as I went on to use my Success Behaviours and Healthy Thinking to ride the next tidal wave — my venture capital ride.

Believe in yourself.

Check that your thoughts are true.

Get the job done in spite of your most ill-informed but well-meaning detractors.

Make sure your thoughts are healthy.

Chapter 4

Venture capital — the second tidal wave

My next business was also to win awards and was successful in raising millions of dollars in venture and start-up capital. I had not anticipated, however, the time, energy and family peace that this wave of technology start-up would consume. While exciting and rewarding, it was the tidal wave of intense work that swept away my family as I knew it.

The concept involved providing a central database, like Internet banking, for medical records and providing medical consultations over the Internet. I called it Doctor Global and founded the website, www.doctorglobal.com. One medical establishment reacted by calling me a snake-oil pedlar. Rather than thinking they were picking on me, I thought they were ill-informed. They were. I could have picked a fight but I chose to inform them, which I did.

I have always practised safe medicine and have never prescribed narcotics except in exceptional circumstances in face-to-face consultations. I found it bizarre that the establishment would think that just because the Internet was involved we would be shipping drugs to people we did not know. One of the first things you agree to do as a doctor is to do no harm.

Despite very harsh publicity and fears by the medical establishment I went ahead. Arguably, I did the first ever consultation with a patient in the world, using medical records, advice and credit card data transferred over the Internet. The publicity gradually became favourable, with a *60 Minutes* documentary and many other favourable newspaper and magazine articles about the company.

I remember giving advice to a woman in Boston. Her husband was very sick and she was worried. He was in hospital and she wanted to take him somewhere else. I didn't need to ship her any drugs. She needed reassurance and I gave her the right questions to ask the specialists that were looking after her husband. I told her the reason she was seeking a second opinion at 3 a.m. from someone on the other side of the world was because she felt disenfranchised from the first opinion.

The next morning, in a non-threatening way, she asked the doctor the questions I had given her. The doctor on the other side of the world sat down and talked to her. He answered her questions and she became part of the process. At 3 a.m. she had been frightened, wanting to pull all the tubes out and go somewhere else. By the morning she was calm and happy that her husband was on the road to recovery. She sent me an email thanking me for my support and advice.

Despite the detractors, I knew I was right. What is good for the patient is good for the business. It is not good for unseen patients to be supplied with drugs and I am sure there are plenty of operators out there that have shipped Viagra, Xenical and other lifestyle drugs with no thought of the consequence of getting it wrong. The challenge I had was to convince investors and the medical profession that I was not one of those pariahs.

The stakes were high. I had been told that the US senate had discussed my company and there were chances I could get sued if I gave the wrong advice. Lawyers and attorneys suggested that I would be a revenue model for those wanting to sue me. To get medical indemnity insurance was expensive and time-consuming. I pressed on in the belief that what I was developing would help people and that it made sense.

To this day I have never done anything dishonest and my intention is always to help people. This may seem naive. Perhaps I should have been more defensive. But my boyish trust was rewarded with nothing but praise from patients all over the world. They thanked me for helping them come to grips with their illnesses and for giving them advice. No one sued me.

The amount of capital needed to fuel the website and technical development grew. I had raised tens of thousands of dollars from friends and family because they believed in and trusted me.

The dotcom bubble was expanding and we were part of it. There was no turning back. The New Zealand Medical

Council, which could remove my licence to be a doctor, wrote some guidelines for Internet consultations. They asked to meet me and adopted some of my own code of conduct that I had written in the absence of any world standards for Internet consultations. Being first, I wrote my own and published them on the site. More doctors joined the site, among them my best friend Dr William Peters, who helped with design, development and funding.

Not only was I trying to build a world-class, world-first medical software company, I was trying to do it from a remote rural community and a small provincial town. I was working full time as a doctor, seeing patients to keep money coming in to feed the family. I was working nights in my attic on my computer writing business plan after business plan and trying to convince investors that this was the way of the future.

I had a three-year-old daughter and a two-year-old son and my marriage was suffering. I had spent so much time and money, not all of it mine. I was on a huge wave and there was no turning back. I thought everything would come right once I got the venture capital. I could drop my medical practice and concentrate on running the business. I was wrong.

I was putting my entire worth on the line as the business developed. For example, we needed a programmer, as we had been using another company for our web-building. I heard about a Colombian doctor who had done some programming and who was living in a city four hours' drive away. He couldn't register as a doctor in New Zealand but had left Colombia because of the endemic terrorism and political unrest.

I rang and invited him down. Dr Libardo Suarez drove to our city and I gave him a tour and told him it was a good place to bring up children. I liked him.

I phoned my friend William who suggested I employ him. I had run out of money but I remortgaged my house, not for the first time, and phoned Libardo. I offered him the job. He accepted on the spot, quit his job and told his family that he was moving to Taranaki on Monday, which was three days later.

I put the airfare on my credit card, told him to be at the airport at 9.30 Monday morning and I would send the only other company employee to pick him up. (The office was now located at the back of my medical practice.)

Monday came and the PA returned from the airport empty-handed. Where was Libardo? He wasn't on the plane!

I rang him between patients. The poor guy had said goodbye to his family and had driven half an hour to the airport to find there was no ticket for him. The airline had booked him the following week but he didn't know that. He had driven back to see his family. I told him to get back to the airport and get on the next plane. He did and still works for Doctor Global four years later.

With increasing programming came increasing web traffic and publicity. My wife was stressed with having to look after young children and even when I was at home my thoughts were on the business. I suggested she go on holiday to Indonesia with her niece for a break for a couple of weeks and I would look after the kids. She did. It wasn't easy for either of us. By now I had almost $100,000 of my friends' and my own money riding on the business.

I live in a farmhouse with chickens, cows and pigs on the farm. I had grown up in the city and used to hassle my parents to shift to a farm as I wanted the space of the country. Live your dreams!

My wife was overseas and I was attempting to change a nappy in-between doing an Internet consultation when the phone rang. It was the major New Zealand television network wanting to do a story for the national news that night. They'd be at my house in an hour.

The house looked like a war zone. I ran around trying to make it look tidy and, in the process, inadvertently left the back door open. I had my daughter under one arm, when my son for some inexplicable reason vomited on the floor at the precise moment the television crew van lumbered down the drive. To all those parents with young children I'm sure you know the feeling.

I rushed for a towel, my bare foot hit something very slippery on the polished floorboards and I flew into the air. The chickens had got in through the back door and my foot had hit some fresh and very smelly chicken shit. Oh for a city condominium and carpet. I broke the fall with my butt and cushioned my daughter's fall with my ample tummy. The vomit and chicken dropping were quickly swept away as the television crew knocked on the door. I'm not so sure about the smell. Maybe they were polite, but they never mentioned the odour as they filmed away. That night the phone went crazy as I was on national television news.

As the business grew I travelled the world. I went to the US looking for venture capital. After Phoenix and San Diego, I toured Silicon Valley in San Francisco. I met with the Kleiner Perkins executives, who had funded Amazon.com and, I believe, Netscape among others. I remember one of the managing partners, Joe Lacoub, saying that Doctor Global was one of the best ideas he had seen but there were too many ideas and to simplify it. He asked me how much for one of my Doctor Global shirts and I quipped, '$3,000,000 and you can have the company for free!' He laughed and replied, 'Get back to me when it is more simple!' I remember seeing what looked like containers of business plans headed for what looked like a large shredder. I thought at least we avoided that.

I went to Asia as investors wanted to join the dotcom bubble. WebMD was starting and they had similar ideas. I wondered if I had written or given away too many business plans and if non-disclosure documents were worth the paper they were written on.

I hadn't doubted my vision at any stage. Looking back I bit off a huge challenge. To try to get doctors and institutions to share their health data through one server is a big ask.

I had never been to Europe. Microsoft was having an

e-health conference in Belgium called MS HUGE. Translated it means Microsoft Health Users Group, Europe. It was huge, and in a place called Brugge. It had, it seemed, 1000 participants. It was a bit daunting not speaking the language and catching trains on my own to places I had never been. But what was the worst thing that could happen? I could get lost. So what?

From being a lonely voice in the New Zealand wilderness, I was among fellow visionaries at the Microsoft conference. While no one was doing exactly what I wanted to do, they nodded their heads in agreement at my concept. I went home and decided to rebuild everything on a Microsoft platform. Eventually I secured significant venture capital, so with that in the bank, I threw a party to celebrate. People came from far and wide.

As I dropped the last person off at the airport our chief information officer turned up at my house. He told my wife that now the venture capital had arrived she would never see me as I would be so busy. I don't know if that was the straw that broke the camel's back but he was right.

Getting venture capital only proves you have a good idea. Then you have to make it work. Neither my wife nor I had prepared for that, and with two young children we were exhausted anyway. She told me she was leaving and did so on 1 July 2000. That was her exit strategy.

I took the two venture capitalists to the airport and told them my tragic news. They looked concerned but said that I would be all right. I wasn't all right. It was as if my world had ended.

Not long after the television programme *60 Minutes* aired its documentary on me.

> By any standards Dr Tom is an extraordinary person. He's a mad-keen surfer, flies a Vampire jet, was a forest ranger, has a first class honours degree in molecular biology, is a general practitioner and doctor for the Taranaki rugby team, survived a tidal wave in Java and is founder of Doctor Global, an Internet medical service that he passionately believes will improve your health care by seeing your doctor less.
>
> Mike Valentine

Shortly after, *North and South* magazine did a five-page feature on the company, William Peters and myself.

> Tom Mulholland has a seemingly inexhaustible and infectious enthusiasm for seizing opportunity. As is often the case with such people, who turn life's lemons into lemonade to sell at a profit, any disaster becomes an adventure.
>
> Deborah Coddington

That was to be a prophetic statement with regard to the tidal wave. Little did the journalist know that I was facing disaster. However, like lemons to lemonade, the break-up of my family was to be the beginning of Healthy Thinking.

The birth of someone or something else often follows

death. From a fire that destroys the jungle, new shoots grow. I saw the documentary on television and read the magazine article yet felt nothing but sadness. I employed a nanny and struggled for six months to run my house, my children and the business. Looking back, what I was really struggling with was my emotions.

I had to give a presentation in Australia and chair a major conference. I was distraught. I had phoned my wife back in New Zealand. She had told me that one of my best friends was visiting her. He was playing with my kids and they were having fun.

I was thinking in an unhealthy way. I began to look ahead through a crystal ball distorted by my unhealthy thoughts. Rather than think she was reassuring me that she and the children were fine, I began to see my friend shifting in, taking over my family and living happily ever after.

I cried for hours and was totally and absolutely miserable. I then had to front up to chair the Sydney conference and give my lecture. I remember it went well and the audience laughed as I made wisecracks and acted like I was in control. As soon as the show was over I retreated to my room and began to cry again.

There was a knock on the door. It was a friend who had with him Professor Peter Yellowlees, an eminent psychiatrist recognised as a world expert on Internet and Telemedicine. I thought they had come to lock me up.

No, the professor wanted to meet me and ask a favour. As the conference was so popular there was no accommodation left. Would I mind sharing my room as

I had the only spare bed!

That must rank as one of the longest nights of my life. I had to talk Internet medicine, investment and a range of other subjects. All I wanted to do was to tell him I thought I was clinically depressed. All I wanted was my family back and I didn't care if I was alive or dead. I couldn't sleep. I lay awake all night listening to the professor breathing.

I was unhealthy in my mind, not my normal self, and William suggested I step down as CEO of Doctor Global. This was a blow at least as tumultuous as the first tidal wave and a huge knock to my confidence. It left me as battered and bruised as the first wave, only this time emotionally.

Doctor Global had been in my head for every waking moment for nearly four years. I was also aware that some entrepreneurs stay at the helm too long. A different set of skills was needed so I stepped aside. William took over as CEO. The dotcom bubble burst, technology stocks crashed, as did thousands of entrepreneurs and investors worldwide. We found another CEO and I worked on a consultancy basis for the company, which has continued in one form or another to this day. I was convinced that we would survive and do well as our business model made sense.

What goes up may come down.

Always plan your exit strategy.

Chapter 5

Despair and depression — the third tidal wave

While I was fully involved with Doctor Global, a large US health management group with eight million patients had committed to using Doctor Global software and the deal is, in fact, now completed. It took the hard work of programmers and subsequent chief executive officers and chief financial officers after me but the idea has worked and is working. I thank them for their efforts.

I look at the software we built as part of the dream and vision that I created and no one can ever take that away. That in itself is more satisfying than the money, believe it or not. Like Sir Tim Wallis, the helicopter pilot mentioned earlier, my divorce was a factor that proved I wasn't the CEO I or other people thought I was, but the vision of Doctor Global was still a sound one.

At one stage my shareholding in the business had potentially been worth over $6,000,000. Another way I think of it is that I got a $6,000,000 education. Since then I have been appointed to an interim board of a government group called Health Intelligence. I go to meetings and conferences now and people are either talking or making the reality of my original concept happen.

However not only my deterioration in mental health but also a number of other factors were to cause the original seed investors, including myself, to be reduced to homeopathic quantities in terms of shareholder dilution.

The major technology crash and the dotcom bubble bursting like a boil meant finding investment in technology was almost impossible. The company had signed a term sheet for millions of dollars as the second round of investment but the money never came. We were faced with insolvency or dilution. We took the lesser of two evils and were diluted.

I couldn't go out of the house for weeks as I felt I had let everyone down as the share price plummeted. I thought I was a failure and that people would resent me. But was that thought true? The company was still going and we were building the product. We were successful; it's just that the share price was terrible. We hadn't folded and although arguably no one lost more money and time than me, it wasn't entirely my fault. I had done what I had been advised to do and thought was best for the company at the time and handed over the reins. Almost all shareholders have been supportive, philosophical and understanding, and I found out who my real friends were.

I had the choice to resent the new major shareholders or take the view I still had 500 million shares in the company. I still work for Doctor Global on a contract basis and still believe in the original concept. Throwing my toys out of the cot would have had no beneficial gain and may have even been detrimental.

I believe that those who have invested in and supported me will be rewarded in new and significant ways and I have not forgotten them. The best thing I can do is learn from the dilution experience and avoid such risks in future. Without the pain of being diluted and the pain of my divorce I wouldn't be as happy as I am now and be in the position to help so many people.

I remember once reading that Thomas Edison invented 9999 ways not to make a light bulb work before he found one that did work. He didn't regard all those trials as failures. They were still discoveries — of ways that did not work.

You have to pick yourself up and go again. Without that experience and the dismal period of depression I am about to describe, I wouldn't have discovered Healthy Thinking and started The Attitude Doctor.

The spiral of malcontent began. From standing aside from the company in which I had invested so much of myself, and dealing with the break-up of my family, my thinking became increasingly unhealthy and destructive. It nearly killed me.

A huge tidal wave of despair eventually crashed down on me. One day I just stopped. I was supposed to work a week of nights in the emergency department at the hospital in which I had been working since going part time for Doctor

Global. I phoned in sick and said I couldn't work any more.

That sickness was to last three months. For the first time in my career I didn't feel safe to make decisions about other people's lives. I couldn't sleep and I couldn't stop crying. I got a medical certificate and a prescription from my doctor and began to realise for the first time just how inadequate the treatments being offered were for the depths of depression in which I found myself.

The first day after stepping down as CEO had been a nightmare. I was used to 100 emails a day, 30 phone calls and a clutter of activity. It all stopped and it was like I was living someone else's life. There was silence. I had gone from being very important to being nobody in a day. It was scary and I panicked. I had failed. Phone calls were few and far between.

The second day was also a nightmare. In fact, the first six weeks were. Each day I took my anti-depressant and waited for it to kick in. I did exercise and walked the dog for an hour each day through country streams and forests. I did what I had been telling patients to do for years. From experience I knew that I had to get better but there was always that doubt. I think I know now why people take their own lives. If you thought you were going to feel like that for the rest of your life you would want to end it. Exercise is good because it stimulates endorphins, which make you feel good. It also gave me the sense that I was going somewhere.

I had always been successful and had rarely experienced

failure. Almost anything I had wanted I had got from hard work and setting goals. Yet now I was reduced to the lowest low of my life.

One of the defining moments in my period of depression was when I recognised that I was allergic to it. It would be difficult to find someone more motivated than me to beat the depression. I hated it so much.

I didn't want to be paralysed. I wanted to get better and have fun. I missed that. My usual persistence and success orientation helped. I read countless books on cognitive behavioural therapy and rational emotive therapy. Even as a doctor and scientist I found most of them complex and confusing.

I spent much of that three months reading as well as exercising and taking the prescribed medication which, though I'm sure helped restore my serotonin levels, didn't fix my unhealthy thinking.

Healthy Thinking can treat the feelings of despair triggered by unhealthy thinking. Continuous exposure to unhealthy thoughts may lower serotonin and other mood chemicals leading to deeper depression. Our environment interacts with our genes to create ourselves. Healthy Thinking can alleviate much of the potential environmental harm.

I don't know if I will ever get depressed again. I hope I don't. If I have a biochemical deficiency and I again need medication I will take it but I also know that Healthy Thinking will continue to act as my strongest weapon in helping to prevent it.

Thankfully, as the medication and exercise regime began to work, my mind began to function a little closer to the level of reasoning I was used to, and my confidence began to return. I started to sleep again. Thinking at 2 a.m. is in the most part unhealthy. If you regularly wake at 4 a.m. it can be a sign of depression, which can be due to low levels of serotonin and other neurotransmitters.

For a while the lack of phone calls continually depressed me. I felt alone. In fact, depression has been described by some as a disease of loneliness. Gradually I started to apply some reason to the situation.

I started to think that it was a good thing to have some space. I changed my thinking to: no messages meant peace and quiet — I could get on with another project, like writing a book. I used to complain that I had too many phone calls and now I was feeling bad that I didn't have enough.

Feeling bad about not getting any phone calls wasn't going to change anything, I reasoned. If I wanted more phone calls I just had to ring people and leave messages on their answerphones. At least half of the people would ring back within a day. So if I wanted, say, five calls a day I would phone ten people!

The point is that I could control what was going on by controlling my attitude. The number of phone calls I would receive in a day was now much more in my control.

However, there was still something missing. I wasn't thinking right. I was still having unhealthy thoughts that would easily tip me back into the darkness. The loss of my family unit was like the death of a family member. This single thought was paralysing me and keeping me from enjoying life. I asked my insurance company about cognitive behavioural therapy, something you touch on at medical school. They agreed to send me to Auckland to see a new psychologist experienced in this approach.

As an aside, I had vicariously experienced severe depression some years before, through a friend of mine, Dr Mike Cox, to whom this book is dedicated, and I didn't want to take it too lightly. I had returned from working in San Francisco General Hospital in the AIDS ward and ER.

On the way back I had travelled through Central America with my surfboard, had worked as a doctor in an oyster town called Bluff (so I could eat oysters), climbed mountains, skied off peaks and tried hang-gliding and other extreme sports.

Once back, I spent a fantastic week ski-mountaineering with this good friend, Dr Mike Cox. We had a great week in the mountains and stood on the main divide where Sir Edmund Hillary had cut his mountaineering teeth. We climbed and skied our butts off. Each morning at 4 a.m. we would wake and ski across the creaking glacier with our skis in the moonlight to the sound of huge ice-cliffs falling off New Zealand's highest peak, Aorangi/Mt Cook.

We put on our crampons and climbed up the main range. We could see the sun rise from the sea on the east coast and see it set in the sea on the west coast on the same day from the same spot.

Unfortunately, some years later, Mike's thoughts and depression became too much and he took his own life. There aren't many days that go by when I don't think what a talented, fun and successful guy he was and miss his company. He was a top white-water canoeist, extreme skier, had attended the world hang-gliding champs and was a good doctor.

I have had other friends and patients who were successful and full of life but who had dark days and decided to end it. Some tried to get help. Others did it on the spur of the moment, leaving no clues. Some had run out of medication.

In my experience of being a doctor and studying and attending suicides, depression and unhealthy thinking kills people, not Prozac. As a medical student I had researched all police crisis team files on suicide over the previous ten years and wrote a paper called 'Is Suicide Predictable or Preventable?'

I found that a significant percentage of suicides were of depressed people. Many were impulsive acts by young males who had been rejected by their girlfriends or who had a significant loss.

I didn't want to end up like them and having thought about ending it all, I went off to see the new counsellor. He was great. I was hungry for a cure and he sent me in the right direction.

Previous counsellors I had seen had made little difference. Some of them said, 'So I think I hear you say you are miserable.' 'Yes, I am,' I would say and want to add, 'Now fix me!'

But they couldn't and didn't. Depression often isn't that straightforward. I think the way to tell if a certain treatment isn't working is if you aren't getting any better. And I wasn't!

I should emphasise that it is difficult to practise Healthy Thinking if you are low in a chemical called serotonin in the brain or clinically depressed. In my experience with moderate to severe depression, anti-depressants and Healthy Thinking work best together. Sometimes Healthy Thinking may get you off medication quicker too. Healthy Thinking can be described as a form of cognitive behavioural therapy (CBT) for those of you who understand what that is. I find it easier to teach people to think in a healthy way than to say I am prescribing CBT.

If you have symptoms of low mood, irritability, poor concentration and memory, changes in weight or appetite, poor sleep or early morning wakening (without good reason), suicidal thoughts, loss of libido, unusual aches and pains, lack of energy or motivation or you don't enjoy the things you used to, like music or activities, you should see your doctor. The new anti-depressants help restore serotonin and could save your life. If you had all those symptoms day in and day out, would you not feel suicidal if you thought there was no cure?

Depression can be a mix of unhealthy thinking and low levels of serotonin and other neurotransmitters. I am sure there are also other factors such as sunlight and temperature. There is, for example, a condition known as SAD, Seasonal Affective Disorder.

As a doctor I may have written thousands of prescriptions to treat depression. I have seen the full range of outcomes, from remarkable results to little effect. I have always been aware of the stigma of depression in our society. I have told patients that they should think of it like diabetes or asthma in the head, not be ashamed that they have a chemical imbalance and take their medication. Most do and most do get better. If I told my diabetic patients to throw away their insulin and make it themselves I would be called crazy and be negligent. Sometimes you need to replenish your serotonin levels and for this you definitely may need medication.

However, over the years I have seen more and more people prescribed anti-depressants. Why? They certainly can save people's lives and do. But are anti-depressants now over-prescribed as a cure all? I remember when I was prescribed them. I was grateful for something, anything to change the way I felt, to help me sleep. I was clutching at straws. But I knew there had to be something else.

I remember a patient describing the same feeling to me once. He would wake up in the morning, look out the window and go, 'What a nice day.' Then he would remember, 'I'm a broken, shattered man!' (He had broken up with his girlfriend.) It took a few seconds for the thought to kick in and when it did, it created the feelings. A minute would take an hour, an hour would take a day and a day would take a week.

I asked him why he felt like that. He said he loved her and couldn't live without her.

I then asked him if that thought was true. He had lived without her before. In fact he had lived well for 32 years without her. He had met her when he was 32 and he was only 33!

'Rather than being a disaster,' I said, 'this gives you an opportunity to grow and develop, to sort yourself out and examine why your partner left. It will be tough for a while but if you can sort yourself out you may get back together. You may find someone or something better! If you change the thought you may even feel excited rather than despondent.'

Those words came back to haunt me. If you are low in serotonin it is harder to think in a healthy way, though it's not impossible. Having prescribed thousands of doses of anti-depressants it was time to get a dose of my own medicine. I waited for the effect. From experience I knew it would be at least two weeks.

I was a now a closet depressive. I didn't want to tell anyone, as I was ashamed. How could this happen to me? I was a doctor. I should know better. It was hard to tell myself what I had happily told patients in the past: that it was just a chemical imbalance or I had a flu in my head. For a while, I still felt like a loser for being depressed and tried to hide it.

I might lose my pilot's licence, my occupation, my friends, my children, and my respect. I had already lost my self-respect for losing my wife and job as CEO of my company. I called my depression stress, then serotonin deficiency syndrome. These names seemed a little less stereotyping than depression and I didn't want to be labelled.

Today I openly talk about my depression. I am amazed at how many people understand and say, 'I'm not surprised. I would have too.' I thought I would be a leper, but some people seemed to admire me for talking about it. I had been thinking in an unhealthy way.

What would they think of a depressed doctor — a failure? A friend and colleague thought I was unwell writing a book about it and exposing my personal life and dark times! But I felt people should know that if I could get depressed, anyone could. It took me some time to have the courage to come out of the depression closet. Even now I have colleagues saying I should hide it. But I believe this feeds the stigma that depression is a weakness. We don't ask diabetics to hide their sugar issues.

I hid my depression for a long time. As I developed Healthy Thinking I taught more and more patients the techniques. Today I tell patients I have been where they are now. They often laugh when I describe how I felt. You may think depressed people can't laugh. Some can. It might be only for a second but I tell them there is light that isn't a train at the end of the tunnel. When you are depressed it is like being in a dark hole or a grey mist with no way out. If you had no hope you would want to kill yourself.

The pain of depression is severe. If you haven't been

there it's hard to understand. Just like if you are a man it is hard to fully understand the pain of childbirth or child death. I may be wrong but the pain and agony on mothers' faces when I have told them that their child has died is different from the pain on the faces of the fathers.

I remember being so depressed that I wanted to die. It was horrible. I had little children and I knew I couldn't do it. I had seen the effects of suicide on many other people: parents, children and friends. I didn't want to kill myself and in so doing hurt anyone else or set out to teach them a lesson. I wanted to end the misery I felt. I was sick of feeling that way.

In the past I had worked in a morgue doing autopsies. I had seen the look of shock and disbelief on the faces of young people who had taken their own life. It looked as though they had realised they had made an impulsive mistake. They realised when it was too late.

As stated previously, my research had shown that many were impulsive acts by young males who had suffered hurt or rejection. Many weren't depressed: they were angry and hurt. Others had been chronically depressed and were sick of the pain.

My motivation had increased and I saw the new counsellor in Auckland three times. The words that hit me between the eyes like a thunderbolt were, 'Just because your wife left, are you going to let that ruin your whole life?' Suddenly these simple words brought home to me the fact that I had become fixated on the past — what was but was no more — and not the future. I needed to let go and move on. Good point! I hadn't previously thought of it like that.

I then went and saw the Dalai Lama. I remember him saying how if he thought about being exiled from Tibet in a negative way it could drive him mad. He hadn't seen his land or relatives in a long time and, if he thought about that too much, he would be miserable. However, being the Dalai Lama in exile had opened so many doors. He had travelled, taught peace, and more people knew about Tibet and being peaceful as a result.

Maybe this is how I can turn a lemon into lemonade, I thought. I began to look at ways I could grow and learn and help others in the same predicament. My divorce had opened new doors for me and I could do a lot more.

Recently I saw a patient who had been on a sickness benefit for 20 years. I asked him why he couldn't work. He told me that he had a severe form of depression. I told him that I knew doctors, lawyers, musicians and politicians who suffered the same illness but still had jobs. He was on regular medication and had been stable for a number of years. I told him that he could work, maybe not as an airline pilot, but neither could diabetics or epileptics. He had a similar chemical imbalance.

I suggested he had just lost his confidence and that he could still be a valuable member of society. He shook my hand and thanked me for being the only doctor who had taken an interest in his situation and not labelled him a failure owing to his illness. Of course I'm not the only doctor who would have treated the patient this way, but he walked out determined to get a job. He already had a plan. I took him off the sickness benefit and he was happy about it. He started thinking in a healthy way.

If you are suffering symptoms of depression,
don't be afraid to seek quality professional help.
It is important if you want to feel better.
It may save your life.

Part two

Techniques of Healthy Thinking

Part two

Techniques of Healthy Thinking

Chapter 6

Unhealthy

If I were to ask you to be as angry or stressed as you possibly can right now, how are you going to do it?

You will have to think of an event or a trigger that makes you feel angry or stressed: perhaps your boss ignoring you in the corridor or your husband forgetting to put the rubbish out. The point of this is that:

Thoughts create emotions.

You cannot have an emotion without first experiencing a thought. It is impossible.

Sometimes the thought happens so quickly that you don't recognise it or see it. For example, if you were walking through a bar and someone slapped you in the mouth and you thought he or she did it on purpose you are likely to be angry. You may react by hitting out, depending how big and strong the other person was relative to you! Or, you may choose to do nothing depending on your attitude to violence and the need for self-preservation.

However, if you thought that the person was a cerebral palsy sufferer or was having an epileptic seizure, or that the hit had been an accident, you are more likely to feel quite a different response. Rather than hitting, you may even offer help.

So the same trigger can cause different emotions by having a different thought attached. My years of being a doctor and helping people have taught me that most unhealthy emotions are caused by unhealthy thoughts. If you practise and have developed Healthy Thinking, then you are likely to experience emotions like contentment, happiness and confidence. If, however, your thinking is unhealthy you are likely to feel guilty, jealous, resentful and angry.

Unhealthy thinking is inefficient; it is a waste of time. These days people often ask me how I am so happy and get so many things done. The answer is Healthy Thinking. I can honestly say I spend less than one minute per week feeling any of what I call the ten unhealthy emotions: stress, anxiety, resentment, rejection, sadness, anger, disappointment, frustration, guilt and jealousy.

As soon as I feel one of these emotions I do my Emotional Algebra. By identifying my unhealthy thinking and changing or stopping my thoughts, I can switch quickly into healthy and productive modes of thinking.

If you or your employees feel unhealthy emotions for 30 percent of the working day this is at least a 30 percent loss in efficiency. Unhealthy thinking can lead to large loss in productivity, decreased sales, an increase in personal grievances, lost time, injury, illness and dissatisfaction.

Once you discover and believe that changing your thoughts will change the way you feel, and you learn to control your thoughts, you are halfway there.

Thoughts create feelings, so if you change your thoughts you will change the way you feel.

Write down what percentage of the day you spend in each of these ten unhealthy emotions.

	Percentage (%)
Anger	....
Anxiety	....
Disappointment	....
Frustration	....
Guilt	....
Jealousy	....
Rejection	....
Resentment	....
Sadness	....
Stress	....
Total	....

This is at least how inefficient you are or your business is. Whatever percentage is left isn't going to be fully functional either if it is affected by such negative feelings. Imagine how much time and energy you would free up if you could use Emotional Algebra to virtually totally eliminate the damage that can be done by unhealthy emotions.

The increased time and energy available can make you more successful. You will be more productive and your physical health may improve as your mental health improves. You will be able to focus and achieve goals more easily.

Chapter 7

Emotional Algebra

If you can count to three then you can do this!

Once I had figured out that thoughts create emotions, I had part of the equation. I started to use a formula for achieving my goals.

Trigger + Thought = Emotion

When you feel an unhealthy emotion, subtract the trigger so you can identify the thought.

Emotion – Trigger = Thought

Remember the earlier example about being hit in the face? See pages 79–80 if you feel you need to refresh your memory.

Perhaps the hit was the trigger for an immediate thought, 'I am being attacked'. But before deciding how to react I needed to analyse my thought.

1 Was it true that I was being attacked?

Here is a list of thoughts I could have used to explain the slap.

- He was attacking me.
- As I am a big man, he was challenging me to a fight.
- He was a cerebral palsy sufferer.
- He was having a fit.
- He was telling a story and accidentally hit me as he described the size of the fish he had caught.
- He assumed I was someone else.
- He was a friend playing around.

In reality, it turned out that the man was telling a fish story and hit me accidentally. I was not being attacked, as I had first thought. I had initially chosen an unhealthy thought.

2 Did my original thought help me achieve my goal?

No, it didn't. My goal was to have a relaxing time in the bar, so ending up in a fight was not going to assist that goal.

3 Was the unhealthy thought worth it?

No, it wasn't. It didn't assist my enjoyment or lead to anywhere other than unhealthy emotions, so the thought was better stopped or changed.

Once you identify an unhealthy thought you can elect to stop it, deal with it later, change it, or forget it. If you want to change it, then you need to understand the following equation.

Attitude + Behaviour = Goal

Or said another way:

	Select the attitude
then	*action the behaviour*
to	*achieve your goal.*

I teach people to set a goal then select the attitude and behaviour they need to achieve it. Or said yet another way:

Goal – Behaviour = Attitude

As each thought can create a different emotion and behaviour it can lead you to many different outcomes. You make a decision that will possibly affect the next hour, week or years of your life.

If I had not done my Emotional Algebra on the slap on the face and realised that, as the blow was an accident it need not be taken further, the whole situation could have ended up much differently.

I had seven possible thoughts that could have led to seven different behaviours and outcomes. I could have:

- looked for his medical alert bracelet
- organised a brain scan
- rolled up my sleeves
- called the police
- knocked the man out
- smiled, accepted the man's apology and moved on
- given him a hug.

If each outcome creates another seven possible decisions and outcomes, life can go in many different directions. For example, if you have ten triggers a day that can each have seven thoughts and outcomes that means:

7 x 7 x 7 x 7 x 7 x 7 x 7 x 7 x 7 x 7
= 282 million choices every day.

Your life could go in 282 million different directions in a day!

You can choose which direction your life goes on any day by:

	changing your thoughts
then	*selecting your attitude*
and	*adopting a behaviour.*

For example, you could:

1. Set the alarm and wake up early.
2. Drive to the supermarket.
3. Meet a friend.
4. Go for coffee to their place.
5. Meet a new friend and get invited to a party.
6. Drive to the city.
7. Turn left down a new street.
8. Find a new shop.
9. Buy a stunning outfit.
10. Go to the party and meet the most beautiful woman or man on the planet, fall madly in love and live happily ever after.

Or you could:

1. Not set the alarm and wake up late.
2. Walk to the shop.
3. Buy a lottery ticket.
4. Walk home.
5. Read a book and become inspired to do one of seven things depending on the book you chose.
6. Dig the garden.
7. Fall asleep, wake up and decide to do one of seven different things.

8 Buy another lottery ticket.

9 Watch the lottery results.

10 Not win a thing or win a little or win a lot.

You could even sit on the chair all day, think millions of thoughts and not move. Remember, though, a dream without action is a hallucination. You can change your thoughts many times and select many attitudes but you need to actually get off your butt and do something to initiate change and achieve your goal.

Before you can select your attitude and adopt success behaviours, you need to eliminate unhealthy thinking.

Chapter 8

Select your attitude

Selecting the right attitude is crucial to achieving success.

For a while I was working in a very busy medical practice. I would have to see sometimes 50 patients per day. Sometimes driving to the office was tiring, thinking about how busy I would be. Sometimes I had only five minutes per patient — not long enough to do a good job. I prefer to see 30 patients in the same amount of time. That way I have more time to communicate and do a better job.

I could have stressed about the day ahead and tell myself and everyone else I didn't like the job. I chose instead to try and enjoy myself as much as possible, and to do the best job possible until we could employ an extra doctor to cover the workload. I would laugh and focus on making everyone's life better, even though I had such a short time with each patient. I took each patient one by one and didn't think about the ones before or the many in the waiting room.

My attitude pulled me through many months of this. However, I decided it was becoming unsafe to see so many patients in one day. As it was a rush and there was a great demand, it would be easy to miss something. For example, I would ask patients if they had anything wrong with their bowel motions. If they said no, then I would move on to another question.

In another clinic with a more manageable workload, I had once asked the same question. When the patient said no, I had asked about going more often than usual. 'As a matter of fact, yes,' came the reply. On further questioning I found that the motions seemed to be very dark and like tar — symptoms that can be an indicator of bowel cancer.

I decided that it was too easy to not 'get to the bottom of things' when I had only five minutes. My goal was to deliver quality medicine. I needed to change my attitude and behaviour to achieve that goal. After meeting with the management of the clinic I decided to leave on safety grounds, among others.

Having been the medical director of a large, busy clinic I have always believed in being positive with patients. I have tried to teach the doctors and other staff to treat everyone as important and to enjoy it. You can have fun at work. It is more rewarding and offers more opportunities. Unhealthy emotions, attitudes and behaviours are damaging in any workplace. Not only does productivity drop off, customers are more likely to complain.

Healthy Thinking takes practice. Even after writing this book I had to remember to select another attitude today, to make work fun for everyone, even the sick.

Once you have identified your goal you need to identify the attitude needed to achieve that goal. It will not always be plain sailing. If you aren't getting the results you want, you could choose one of a number of alternative attitudes. I have highlighted two attitudes here:

The Blame Game	or	**Refuse to be Daunted**
It's all their fault.		What could I do differently?
It's hard to get good help.		I need to train my staff.
The market isn't ready.		I need to develop the concept.
I'm a failure.		That was a valuable lesson.
I lost that contract. I'm doomed!		I have time to refine the process.
How dare they criticise me!		Thanks for the advice!
How would they know?		That's a great idea!
It will never work!		It's going to take a little longer.

You can easily see which attitude will help you achieve your goal.

We change our external clothes every day. Why can't we change what we are like on the inside? You can. If your current attitude isn't working, then change it.

I am amazed at how long people persist with the same

attitude even though it hasn't been working for years. If a sports team loses does it change its strategy? Do the Los Angeles Lakers, Manchester United or the Dallas Cowboys stick with the same defensive plan if they have lost five games by big margins? Do they persist with the same offensive plan if they have scored few points? The coach must change the strategy or risk being changed himself.

Don't be frightened by change.

What goes down can come back up.

As humans we can be creatures of habit. If you aren't used to change or taking risks then start slowly. Instead of watching the same sitcom on television every night, do something different.

- Watch another programme.
- Turn off the television set.
- Play cards.
- Read a book to your kids or yourself.
- Give your partner a massage.
- Learn to play the guitar.
- Write a business plan.
- Join Toastmasters.
- Enrol at university.
- Become a lawyer.

- Publish a book.
- Enter politics.
- Join an Internet chat room.
- Fall asleep.

Remember, your life could go in one of 282 million directions if you change each thought, select a different attitude and assume a certain behaviour. That's what makes life so interesting. We are so obsessed by only one path that we can get distressed if it detours. The trick is to keep changing your thoughts, attitudes and behaviours to keep yourself on track towards your goal.

Gloria applied for a job as the chief executive officer (CEO) of an overseas company. She had always been offered every job for which she had applied. She expected to get the CEO job and had told her friends and family that it was a mere formality. When the phone call came to say that she was unsuccessful she was devastated. She couldn't go out of the house, didn't want to phone her family or friends and was struggling to cope with the rejection. By the time she came to see me she was heavily playing the blame game. She was angry, rejected and disappointed. Add in some jealousy and guilt and her current job was suffering.

We quickly identified the thought driving the emotion. Gloria thought she was a failure because she didn't get the job. She was worried that other people would think the same. She was lying awake at night trying to concoct excuses for not getting the job.

I asked her what her goal was. She said it was to become the CEO of a large multinational. Did her sense of being a failure help her achieve that goal? No! Was the thought worth it? No! Was the thought true? It would be if she persisted with the attitude that she had failed.

What were the possible thoughts Gloria could have chosen for not getting the job?

- She wasn't CEO material.
- They didn't like her.
- Someone better got the job.
- They were looking for a different set of skills.
- She was asking for too much money.
- She didn't have the necessary skills.
- She wasn't ready.
- It wasn't the right job for her.
- She needs more training.
- She was over qualified.

These thoughts had been running through her mind constantly and keeping her awake.

I suggested she contact the recruitment company to determine exactly why she didn't get the job.

A week later Gloria came back to see me. She had been

told that the prospective employers thought she was too entrepreneurial for the job. They thought she would get bored very quickly and leave within six months.

Gloria agreed. We got her back on track, she started her own company and is now doing very well. Not only that, she is enjoying working for herself and enjoying the freedom and challenges that that brings.

She is living her dream rather than dreaming her life. She is now the CEO of a multinational company: the important difference is that she owns the company.

Changing your attitude may not have to be as complex as becoming a CEO. You may want to relate better to your teenagers or pets.

Brian had a dog that would usually deposit large amounts of solid waste (dog pooh) on his front lawn. This infuriated Brian, who had tried all sorts of commercial and other remedies to stop it happening. He had spent a small fortune on chemical and plastic deterrents, gates, collars and behavioural training.

The more Brian resented his dog, the more it poohed on the lawn! Brian began to think the dog was doing it on purpose. I explained to Brian that dogs often deposit after a walk as it stimulates the bowel. I suggested that, rather than avoid the dog, Brian take it for a walk after feeding. I thought that the dog may be frustrated at not being walked.

Brian walked the dog on a regular basis. The dog poohed

on wasteland 20 minutes after the walk started. Brian's asthma improved with the regular exercise and he lost ten kilos in weight. He saved lots of money on deterrents and his lawn is no longer a dog toilet!

If you change your attitude and behaviour you often reap rewards you never imagined.

Susan had a neighbour who was a little tense. He was building a large boat and shed. The noise was distracting with banging and heavy machinery and Susan complained to him. He took offence.

Soon after Susan had a party for some friends. The neighbour stormed over and told her to turn down the music. The neighbour threatened to cut off her power if she didn't.

She lived in the country and had plenty of space. She had given the neighbour plenty of warning and invited him. It was an afternoon garden party and Susan had a band playing.

After he complained Susan thought about her goal. Since it was to have a great party she moved the band inside and opened the doors. She thought the neighbour must have something bad going on in his life. Two hours later the heavens opened and the rain came down in a deluge. The band was safe inside and the party continued. The neighbour unwittingly had done her a favour.

Some months later Susan visited her neighbour. She took him a bottle of wine and said she was sorry for getting upset earlier in the year. She could have chosen to be upset and angry for months. She could have had a battle or a war. She didn't. Who won?

I heard from someone recently that a survey was done in a Palestinian school where a group of eight-year-old girls was asked what they wanted to do when they grew up. Ten percent said they wanted to be suicide bombers. You don't have to be an Israeli rocket scientist to work out that in 12 years you will have some serious security problems.

Half of the girls may change their mind; another ten percent may join them. But either way, unless attitudes change, nothing else will. It is easier to change attitudes than build higher walls or smarter bombs.

You may not be from the Middle East or Middle Earth. Your space may not be threatened by Hamas, the Taleban, invading armies, orcs, or even a neighbour. Regardless of your circumstances 15 years of doctoring has taught me that we are all essentially the same. We all make mistakes and we all seek acceptance.

Once you get your own emotions under control you can deal with those of other people. You can select an attitude of compassion, forgiving and understanding. You can choose an attitude of blame, punishment and condemnation. See which one makes you friends, makes you happier, and more successful.

In the many talks and workshops I have done I usually ask members of the audience to raise their hands if they have never made a mistake. No one has yet put up their hand.

It is my belief that ruling by fear is less productive than showing understanding and encouraging improvement. If you want your employees or children to improve, catch them being good rather than humiliate them for being bad.

Set the goal.

Find the attitude you need to reach it.

Then act on that attitude.

Part three

How I use Healthy Thinking

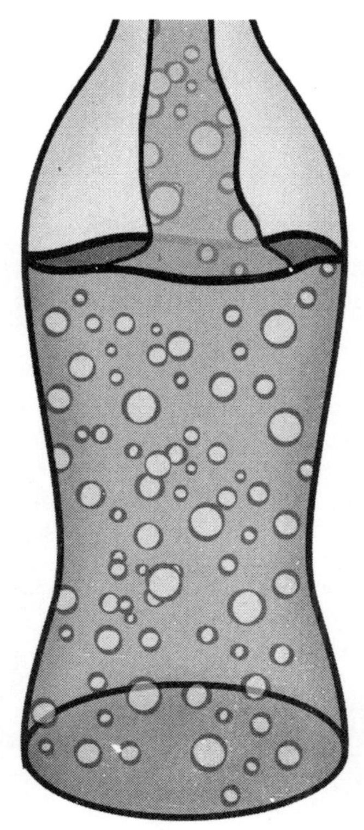

Chapter 9

Practise, practise, practise

Once my shareholding in Doctor Global had been diluted I needed to get another job. As I have mentioned, I went back to being a doctor and doing what I enjoyed, making people healthy. I found, however, that more and more often, as much as prescribing medication, I was able to prescribe Healthy Thinking. More and more people got better. I too stopped taking the anti-depressants that had been prescribed to me by my psychiatrist. My confidence returned and I again began to enjoy life.

Recently I was working in a busy medical practice. The door opened and the nurse walked in — an unusual event, as I don't like to be disturbed when I am with patients. The nurse informed me that the Medical Council of New Zealand was on the phone, which was an even more unusual event as in 15 years of being a doctor no one from the council had ever rung me. The council has the power to take away my licence to practise as a doctor.

(I guess they call it practising as you are always learning.)

I immediately rose from the chair, excused myself to the patient, and headed for the door. I felt my mouth go dry, a lump rise in my throat, my pulse quicken and the gastro-colic reflex start. In other words, I was anxious … very anxious. Why? What was I thinking? I was thinking that someone must have complained or died, or that in some other way I was in trouble. Quickly, I applied a key question to my thoughts:

Was the thought true?
No! It may not be.

I quickly changed the thought to, 'Maybe they are phoning to say I have won the Doctor of the Year competition!'

Immediately I felt excited and couldn't wait to get to the phone. My emotions had changed automatically by changing my thoughts. The voice from the medical council said that they were updating their database and wanted my new mobile phone number. Instead of being relieved I was disappointed. Rather than relief from not being in trouble, it was disappointment from not winning an award.

Now there is no such award that I know of. I had merely changed my thoughts to change my emotions. Imagine if I had not been able to get to the phone. As it was late Friday afternoon I could have spent all weekend worrying about nothing and being anxious about a thought I didn't even know was true.

In my experience most unhealthy emotions come from thoughts that aren't true and the more you practise changing your thoughts, the better you get at it. As with the distant large waves, we often get anxious over events that may never happen. Being anxious is more likely to make them happen than to make them not happen. If I had spent the rest of the afternoon worrying about the medical council phone call, I may have missed an important diagnosis.

Over the years I have seen many patients with problems caused by anxiety about events in the future. One such patient was John, who was worried that he may not get his promotion in a few months. He felt that the promotion would give him the money to buy the house he had promised his wife. His anxiety produced enough acid to cause an ulcer in the lining of his stomach. This ulcer then became a full-thickness hole, which perforated the muscle wall, leaking acid into his abdomen. This caused peritonitis, which made him very sick and I had to do an emergency operation in the middle of the night to find the hole and close it.

As a result, John needed a significant amount of time off work and missed the promotion. He was devastated, but only to find out that his wife was relieved. She hadn't wanted to shift to the bigger house; it was a nightmare to clean and their children were about to leave home!

John's lack of communication had created an unnecessary amount of anxiety and his thought wasn't true. What he feared most came true not because of a lack in his ability as a manager but because of his unhealthy emotions and lack of ability to manage them.

It in turn created some anxiety in me, as it was the first time I had sewn up a perforated gastric ulcer in the middle of the night on my own. I was training to be a surgeon at the time. I changed my thought to, 'If you can't find the hole and close it, you can ring the supervising surgeon. In the meantime, just don't hit anything important with the scalpel!' Both John and I got out of the operating theatre intact. Maybe Healthy Thinking could have prevented the whole procedure.

As a general rule unhealthy emotions tend to be caused by unhealthy thoughts. In my years of experience with patients and myself, most unhealthy thoughts aren't in fact true. Misinterpretation creates a false reality that causes unhealthy emotions. These in turn cause destructive or unhelpful behaviours, which tend to take you further away from your goal.

Now please don't read this book and assume I am saying to stop any medication you are on without consulting your doctor or therapist. It may be dangerous. There are many factors that influence depression. Healthy Thinking is one of them.

Recently a very elderly patient was grumbling about the number of tablets she was taking. I replied:

> Why are you unhappy? You should be grateful that these tablets exist! If they didn't you probably would be dead or in a rest home, not living in your own home and tending your garden. Your parents died at an early age of strokes and heart attacks, and you have high cholesterol

> and high blood pressure. Without medication you would certainly be in trouble. Every day you should wake up and thank the Lord for the tablets.
>
> By resenting them and becoming stressed or missing a few, you are more likely to raise your blood pressure, meaning I'd have to prescribe more. Or you may risk having a stroke. Why do you think people live much longer these days? Sure, it's diet and increased public health like immunisation, clean water and less smoking but medication plays a big part.

The woman looked a little taken aback but saw the sense in my words. By changing her thinking and attitude towards her medication she was more likely to stay healthy. Reducing stress is about changing your thinking and changing your attitude.

Stress is born, lives, and dies between our ears. Learn to be content in the moment and enjoy the excitement of not knowing what may happen next. That's what makes life interesting.

You don't always have to be in control! Try doing something someone else suggests next time even if you think you may not enjoy it. Don't knock it until you have tried it is usually a good point of view (making sure it's safe first!). It is less stressful doing what someone else suggests and you may actually enjoy it and learn something else. This reaps particular rewards in terms of children and partners and will gain you respect and fun!

I have found that human beings often choose the thought that makes them feel the worst about a situation. We imagine the worst. I could choose many thoughts when getting heckled doing comedy. I could shrink and get flustered and take comments personally. That would encourage unhealthy thoughts. I choose to enjoy any heckling and get into an amiable banter.

Here is an example of unhealthy thoughts influencing behaviour.

James' wife didn't come home until very late from a party with friends. James thought she may have been having an affair with someone else. He decided it was probably his friend Karl. This made him jealous, angry and resentful. He felt uncomfortable all night and didn't want to ring her cellphone.

When his wife, Carol, came home he yelled at her and accused her of having an affair. Things began to deteriorate and Carol became withdrawn. She started coming home less as she was resenting James' angry behaviour.

That night of the party, James could have chosen a number of thoughts to explain Carol's lateness (2 a.m.). Each thought would ultimately affect his behaviour. Some people seem to select the thoughts that will cause destructive actions. These actions will take you further away from your goal.

James' thoughts may have been, for example:

- She is having an affair and doesn't love me. I feel angry.

- She's having an affair, still loves me but is making a terrible mistake.
- She's having an affair and doesn't love me. I'm better off without her.
- She is having an affair; now I can have one too.
- She's had too much to drink and is waiting to sober up before driving home.
- The car has broken down.
- Karl is upset. As a good friend she is helping him out.
- She has met her sister and is having a great time.
- Her watch has stopped.
- She has had an accident.
- She is having such a great time, she deserves it and she will come home when she wants.

Each different thought is likely to create a different emotion and possible attitude and behaviour.

In this case Carol was late because she was having such a great time. If James had thought this, Carol was more likely to have felt she had an amazing, supportive husband and been less likely to have an affair. With James' negative reaction, though, she felt like she had a controlling, jealous husband and was distancing herself from him.

Obviously if this partying to all hours of the night was a common occurrence James may have needed a different strategy.

Live in the moment and learn to go with the flow.

**Learn to adapt to new situations
and enjoy different outcomes.**

With further Healthy Thinking, I began to seek out new life and adventure. I was elected to the District Health Board with a turnover of $160 million per annum. I was elected as the chairman of my children's school with a turnover of lots of happy kids. I played my guitar in the culture group and coached my children's rugby team. I wrote a long list of all the good things in my life. I began to enjoy the unexpected.

Life became interesting and I enjoyed the moment and the fun of not knowing what would come next. I was teaching others to write lists of the good things rather than the bad things in life, and I formed the core ideas and objectives of The Attitude Doctor.

So I began to think in a healthy way and looked at the positive side of being divorced. I began to realise that sometimes not getting what you want is a good thing. You just have to realise it.

When I was married I used to come home from work and play with the kids. After three years of being on my own I now interact with my kids. I have been mum, dad, friend, teacher and a range of other things. I know my children and they know me.

I'm not suggesting that everyone should get divorced. It's hard work and is an inefficient way to bring up kids but, if you are, there are plenty of advantages. Rather than trying to change my situation I needed to change my attitude and enjoy the situation I was in. My kids are thriving in sport and at school and have plenty of friends. We are a great family.

Let me give you an example of how Healthy Thinking helped me avoid an angry situation at home, and in so doing, further improved my relationship with one of my children. It's my favourite story using Healthy Thinking so far. Each day brings a new one.

My six-year-old son Thomas was running around his bedroom doing everything except getting into bed. It was late at night and he was supposed to be reading his homework book to me. I was tired after seeing 40 sick patients in the surgery, coming home, cooking dinner and cleaning up. Finally after much cajoling, he got into bed. I opened the book and in a barely audible voice he whispered, 'The man said it was time to ...'

For some reason I'd had enough. I dropped the book, stood up and walked out of the room. He yelled out, 'Dad, you're a dick!' I felt angry and was about to react when I realised I was feeling upset. Time to use Emotional Algebra.

I recognised that I was feeling angry, so I asked myself:

> *What was the trigger?*
> I realised that it was Thomas whispering the first line of his book.

So I asked myself:

What was the thought that was driving my anger?
I realised that I was thinking that he was 'taking the piss out of me', and not showing me the respect that a tired father and teacher deserved.

But was this a healthy thought? Was it true? Did he have something stuck in his throat? Was he choking? Was he getting a throat infection? Did he have a brain tumour? I had just assumed he was being obstructive. He could be taking his last breath and I was having a tantrum.

I asked myself some important questions:

Did it help me achieve my goal of helping Thomas read?
The answer was no!

Did it create an unhealthy emotion?
The answer was yes!
I was feeling rejected and was angry.

Using Emotional Algebra, I could see that the thought I created wasn't worth it.

I walked back into Thomas' room. He sat there looking scared. I'm still bigger than him and calling me a dick is an offence under our home penal system. He looked relieved when I apologised.

'Thomas, I'm sorry. I have had a hard day and I thought you weren't helping me out.'

'That's all right,' he said. 'Dads are human too.'

Pleased at this return of the olive branch I sat down next to him and picked up the book. I looked at the title, which

I had neglected to read earlier. The book was called *The Whisper Boy*. Not only that, the opening line was in italics. My son had been reading perfectly.

I felt sick but relieved. The situation could easily have turned to custard. Instead of doing the maths on my emotions I could have reacted far worse than I did.

The situation may have easily escalated into a confrontation with no winners. We wouldn't have done the reading and I would have lost some respect from Thomas. My perception was my reality and I had made the wrong conclusion. Unhealthy thinking had put me in a position where my emotions could have led to stress and dysfunction.

As it was, by recognising my anger and changing my thoughts and perception I had found the truth. By apologising I had gained more respect and we had a wonderful time reading. It ended with a big cuddle, a happy child and a happy father. I had achieved my goal of reading a story to my son.

Emotional Algebra helps in two ways:

1 It makes you stop when you feel an unhealthy emotion and step aside from the feeling of the situation.

2 Once you disengage to an analytical level it helps to slow the pulse and breathing and focus on solving the problem. If you identify the emotion and then subtract the trigger, you can identify the thought.

The key to the situation with Thomas was that I was

thinking that he was being disrespectful by whispering the opening line of the book. Once I dissected the thought I could then analyse it, to see if it was an unhealthy one.

Life is like a game of chess. The more you look, the more options and opportunities open up. If you move a piece one way, it opens up an exponential number of other moves. Being alive and happy is a result of being able to adapt to change and make the most out of the unexpected. The more you do it, the better you get at it and the more you have fun.

The greater the risk, the greater the return. To use this investment strategy is relaxing. Try doing something you hadn't wanted to do and you may actually enjoy it.

This works really well with children and in relationships, as well as almost any situation life can throw at you. For example, I was with my children and trying to solve the problem of having four spare hours in the city on a wet winter's afternoon before taking them to watch a basketball game. I began to stress because every possibility my analytical mind and memory could think of was a non-starter. Every stop in the car was a dead end. The library was closed, the climbing wall was full, we had seen everything at the movies and even the bowling alley was full.

Sensing my frustration, my children said, 'Dad, why don't we go to Pukekura Park?' (Pukekura is a beautiful park in the middle of our city.)

'No!' I retorted, because that's what dads do when they

aren't in a Healthy Thinking mode.

'Why not?' asked the persistent little helpers in the back.

'Because it's raining,' came my sensible fatherly response!

'But Dad, we've got raincoats,' came the even more sensible little helpers' reply.

Defeated, I agreed. 'Okay, let's go to the park.'

Instantly I felt as if a weight had lifted off my shoulders. I was relaxed and in new territory. I was actually doing something my children had suggested, not something I thought they would like.

I have often thought of life as a river of time and have always found rivers and this metaphor relaxing. So I had jumped into the river of life and the moment to see where it would take me.

We got out of the car and the sun came out. We didn't need our coats. We had the park to ourselves because all the other parents were being 'sensible'. I remembered that I used to be a forest ranger and love showing people the forest.

My children were stunned with my Discovery-channel-type tour of the park, its plants and wildlife. As it turned out, we were having so much fun we were late for the basketball. My children said, 'Dad, that was one of the best days we have ever had!'

It was fun, it didn't cost any money, we got some exercise and it awakened some old and very useful memories. Since then I have adopted the attitude of sometimes trying what my children want to do. Most of the time I have lots of fun but the key is to pick which ideas will work and which ones won't. I am constantly surprised how much fun I have trying things I thought I wouldn't do. Rather than being grumpy because no one wanted to do your activity or it wasn't available, try another choice.

We have extended the wet weather strategy on a number of occasions to good effect. Often we go places on purpose if the weather is slightly dodgy. A recent trip to an animal park in a new city in heavy rain produced amazing results. Once again we were the only ones there, in what is normally a bustling place.

Impressed by our commitment the zookeepers took us for a ride in the truck that fed the animals, and we got to go inside the enclosures that most people never get to enter, feeding the lions lumps of meat, hand-feeding the giraffes and scratching the horn of a rhino!

Last weekend the children and I took off for a bike ride. My eight-year-old daughter asked, 'Where are we going, Dad?'

'Wherever the road takes us,' I replied.

She had a twinkle in her eye and excitedly said, 'I knew you would say that.' It was fun.

One of the hardest parts about being divorced is sometimes being separated from your children.

Healthy Thinking can teach me that this may not be a bad thing. I reasoned that, as I live in an energy province with oil and gas rigs, many dads locally would be spending two weeks on the rig and two weeks off. I'm sure their children love them no less than those who see their parents all the time.

My father spent long periods at sea as a marine engineer when I was a child. Some of my friends' parents were airline pilots. They were away for days on end.

Today I have not seen my children but I have been busy writing this book. Tomorrow I am going to their school to do parent help and help with their maths. Coaching their sports teams keeps me in close contact. This year my daughter and I acted in a play, *Charlie and the Chocolate Factory* by Roald Dahl. We spent three months rehearsing and my son came to nearly all the rehearsals.

We had a fantastic time and it was a great experience. Just because you are divorced doesn't mean you have to be divorced from your children. There are many innovative ways you can stay in contact with them and have an even better relationship than you would have had by living as a dysfunctional family.

One key is to get on well with your ex-partner and in no way run him or her down to your children. Imagine being small and hearing your mother or father criticising the other. It is destructive and in the long run will prove totally counterproductive to achieving your goal of having a close relationship with your children.

I talk to plenty of adults who, even though they are older, find it distressing if their parents are fighting. Remember that if it is confusing for you in a marriage break-up, it is even more confusing for your children.

Some of the unhealthy emotions that surround separation and divorce are guilt and jealousy. It is so easy to end up trying to negotiate your future with thoughts distorted by these emotions.

I think I see far more of my children now than I did before I was divorced. This may seem like a cliché but the time I do spend with them is quality time. I started Doctor Global so I could work from home and see more of my children. The Attitude Doctor allows me to do the same. I work some evenings giving seminars but have days to spend at their school.

I am a full-time motivational speaker and coach. I am living the dream. In two days I am giving another talk. My children are coming to watch. They have been involved in the construction of this book and in finding jokes for my comedy routine.

I decided to come out of the depression closet and write this book. In my community people often tell me I am lucky, successful and wealthy. They have no idea that I was miserable. By telling people will they lose respect for me? Will I become a leper?

It takes a lot of courage to admit to your doctor that you are suffering from depression. It takes even more courage to declare it publicly and yet some ten percent of people will experience at least one depressive episode, feeling bad for more than two weeks with the symptoms described earlier.

Healthy Thinking, I'm sure, will help some of those people. I no longer feel ashamed of how I felt. What doesn't kill you makes you stronger. My patients and clients feel more comfortable if I identify with their problem. I'm not sure if the medical establishment frowns on me telling people about my illness. They wouldn't frown if I told the patient that I had influenza. Why should they frown if I said I had been depressed?

I briefly thought that in taking on sponsored speaking engagements there may be a conflict of interest if the sponsors found out I had been depressed. No, that would be unhealthy thinking. It would not be surprising that someone would get depressed if they lost their marriage and their company in close succession and did not have command of the tools of Healthy Thinking at the time.

When I decided to leave doctoring once again to start this new business — www.theattitudedoctor.com — I felt a certain stress, as I was taking a risk. I was leaving a secure, well-paying job as a doctor in a coastal town near where I live. I began to think, 'What if no one comes and hears me speak? What if no corporate groups want to employ my services as a trainer or no one wants to hear my comedy routine?'

I then thought, 'So what, if no one comes to see me? I can always go back to being a doctor. I could go live with my mother. I could sell everything, buy a yacht and sail around the world.' As it turned out I was in hot demand as a speaker and have been ever since.

Often our stress limits our ability to take risks and to grow. When I started writing this book I thought, 'What if no one reads it? What if it doesn't achieve critical acclaim? What if someone else writes it first? What say it is discarded as irrelevant nonsense?'

It doesn't matter, I decided, because if one person reads the book and it makes that one person's life different it will have been worth it. If I had let my fear of failure limit me, I never would have starting writing. The more I wrote, the more people said they enjoyed it. I began to gain more confidence in what I was doing.

'So what, if no one reads it,' I thought. 'I believe Healthy Thinking is the most powerful thing that has happened to me, and I have done many wild and crazy things and taken plenty of risks. It has been a good experience for me and I want to share it.'

Sometimes not getting what you want
is a good thing.

Go with the flow, enjoy the moment.

Chapter 10

Stand-up comedy

Time for a new goal. I had increasingly thought about being a motivational speaker, focused on the idea that with the right attitude you can do anything. I decided to prove to myself that, with my newfound power of Healthy Thinking, I could go from being miserable to being a stand-up comedian in six months.

This was also part of my plan to get used to an audience and try to make them laugh with original material. Well, at least have a go at it. From being unable to go out of the house to standing up in front of 850 people telling jokes within six months was a great goal. I achieved it through Healthy Thinking, Success Behaviours and the right attitude.

I had spoken at a number of national and international conferences on health. Most people laughed during my presentations and I was getting requests for after-dinner speaking.

I wasn't afraid of large or intimidating audiences, which was a plus. In fact, a few years before I had been at an

America's Cup dinner at which four billionaires were on the panel after dinner. They were Jim Clark, founder of Silicon Graphics, Netscape and Healtheon; Tom Perkins of Kleiner Perkins, the VC company; John Sculley of Apple Computers; and Bill Koch of sailing and business legend. They were a formidable panel, but I stood up in front of a large audience and asked a very direct question, which attracted some attention and led to the securing of the venture capital for Doctor Global.

So I thought having a go at stand-up comedy would be worthwhile. Accordingly, I turned up one day at New Zealand's premier comedy bar, The Classic, in Queen Street, Auckland. The owner, Scott, gave me a slot on a Monday night and I turned up with an entourage of friends, keen, I'm sure, to see me make a fool of myself as I appeared there for my first ever gig.

I must admit to nearly not making it as I had to organise babysitters for my children and it was a lot of work. But I remembered my goal and stuck with it. I was committed, or should that be committable?

The MC on the night was Mike King, New Zealand's best comedian. After a difficult start, me telling him he knew my auntie and him telling me she wasn't his favourite person (in very colourful language), we got on with each other and soon enough it was my turn on stage.

I felt like I was on fire. I threw everything into my performance. This was an opportunity, with some very successful comedians also performing on stage that night, so I took it. I was confident, even ad-libbed and had my first audience ROAR, which I assure you is a very addictive buzz.

I was noticed and my comedy was of a sufficient standard for me to be invited back to do another couple of nights in the January school holidays. I have done some forgettable gigs since — all part of that learning curve. At one stage I thought I was getting worse. I changed my thought to the view that audiences were getting tougher, meaning I worked harder at pleasing them and things came right again.

About a month later, Mike King came to New Plymouth, my home city, as part of his National Pride nationwide comedy tour. Between 800 and 1000 people were expected to his performance at the local Showplace Theatre. His promoter had contacted the local newspaper to see about doing a feature on the upcoming gig. The reporter had asked if I would be performing (I had told her that I had done a gig with Mike King). The promoter suggested I open the show for Mike, and asked me to have an interview with the paper, all in 48 hours.

What was the worst that could happen? No one would laugh.

I said yes, as I normally do, then thought about the consequences later. It was an opportunity too good to miss, I decided. So the article was in the paper. I told some friends who bought tickets and I prepared my routine, all in a day or two.

The big day dawned, Friday, and I was ready but nervous. I was looking forward to seeing Mike again. I wanted to run my jokes past him and see if he thought they were funny or not. I was hoping for some advice.

I rang his road manager, also called Mike, and was disappointed with the response, which wasn't what I was expecting.

'Dr Who?' he asked.

'Dr Tom, who is opening for Mike tonight!' I proudly said.

'No one told me anything,' came the gruff reply. 'Who said so?'

'Ah, Paul, the promoter,' I confidently exclaimed.

'Ring me back at 4 p.m. then.' Click. He hung up.

At 4 p.m., I duly rang back.

'Turn up at 6 p.m.,' came the reply, then click.

He obviously wasn't happy.

So I turned up at 6 p.m. and met Mike and the road manager, who to the uninitiated is an imposing figure. Mike was pissed off.

'This shouldn't have happened,' he barked. 'We are doing a professional show here. We have a routine and Paul never should have done this!'

It was clear that Mike King was really angry about this. Things were not good.

'Oh,' I said, 'I'm sorry. I was just trying to help sell more tickets. If you want, I can flag it and not do it.'

'No, it's in the paper now. You have three minutes!!!'

Well, if I was nervous before, now I was terrified and disappointed. Instead of getting angry, resenting it or feeling rejected, I thought, 'Wow, something else must be going on for them to be so pissed off.' I thought, 'Oh well, three minutes is better than nothing, and I can't go too wrong in three minutes.'

Going on stage with 850 locals who knew me out in front and a pissed-off Mike King and road manager out the back felt like going to the electric chair.

Later, I found out that the whole PA system had blown up and that the WOMAD (World Of Music And Dance) festival was on in town the same weekend so that getting a new sound system was harder than finding a legal-sized abalone (paua) off the Taranaki coast.

My point is that I managed my own internal conflict and understood that another conflict must be happening to cause this situation. Initial disappointment was replaced with pragmatism and I didn't get resentful or feel rejected. I was having enough trouble controlling my anxiety without another three unhealthy emotions on top! I had the right attitude for the situation, adapted to the changed circumstances and learnt a lot from the master of comedy.

The outcome of it all, however, is that I have become friends with Mike King, and have just returned from doing Fiji's first ever stand-up comedy gig with him.

Everyone is a comedian.

Laughter is the best medicine.

Chapter 11

Who needs enemies?

Many people involved in business and in health say to me that feelings of anger and guilt are natural human emotions. They ask why such feelings should be avoided or they say that people can't avoid them. Well, death is also natural and some of us spend a lot of time and money trying to avoid that. On the other hand, some people spend a lot of time and money trying to die early, but that's another story in a later chapter.

We could spend a lot of time debating whether emotions such as anger, jealousy or sadness are good for us and whether they provide a protective benefit. I cannot think of a single example where getting angry and losing your cool with yourself or someone else has any benefit or produces positive long-term health results.

Take road rage, for example. You are late for an appointment. You are in heavy traffic when a male driver cuts you off and makes you catch a red light. You think he did this on purpose, that he has no respect and should be taught a lesson. You run the red light, catch up with the other car and get out of your car to abuse him. Your blood pressure goes up from yelling. You have a small stroke, end up missing your meeting and arrive in hospital instead. To make matters worse, not only do you get a ticket for running the red light, but also the effects of the stroke cause you to lose your job.

Another scenario may have been that you catch the guy, yell abuse at him and then roar off. It turns out that the reason he cut you off was that he was equally in a hurry to get to the same meeting as you, your job interview. As you are the applicant, it's not a good start. Healthy Thinking could have prevented both scenarios.

If you had changed the thought from, 'He did it on purpose' to 'This guy is from out of town and is lost' or maybe 'He's in a hurry to get to the hospital as his wife is having a baby', you may even have sympathy for the guy. You could have given him a wave, then taken the few minutes at the red light to get your composure and focus on the job interview. That way, you get to the interview calm and prepared to find the man you waved at is interviewing you for the job. He sees that you do well under pressure and you get the job.

Conflict can be both external and internal. I define conflict as:

> the gap between our expectation of behaviour
> and actual performance.

In other words, the difference between what we want and what we get.

If you have a large amount of internal conflict, sooner or later it will spill over to cause external conflict, which will affect your environment. Once again, if you don't have your own act sorted then it will be more difficult to have peace in your life and harmonious relations with others.

Recently I was sitting at a red light in my automatic car in a large city I was unfamiliar with. It was rush-hour traffic, which must be an oxymoron. How can you rush when you are bumper to bumper? Maybe it's everyone's thoughts that are rushing, and just imagine what chaos they are likely to be causing. Anyway I leant over to check the map and by mistake my foot eased off the brake. As I was in gear, the car rolled forward and bumped the car in front of me. At first I couldn't work out what had happened. I had no perception of motion at the time and thought the car ahead must have reversed into me.

In a flash, a very large man had leapt out of his car and was advancing towards me like a tank. He had a very angry look on his face. Like a machine gun, his words of abuse spat out, telling me to move back and over to the side of the road. I duly got out of the car to inspect the scene. Now I am 6 foot 3 inches (1.9 metres) tall and weigh 105 kilograms (16.7 stone) and had been a security officer (flash word for a bouncer) for a number of bars while at university. I had also been a forest ranger, can box and was handy pushing a rugby scrum as well. This guy made me look like a dwarf. He was big, *very* big and he was very, *very* angry.

He was almost frothing at the mouth, telling me that I had bent his bumper off the bracket; that it was going to be very expensive; and that he was upset (not quite in those words). His car looked like it had been through a number of wars and had seen better days.

Being a stand-up comedian I thought some humour might diffuse the situation. *Wrong.* I politely told him that the only thing holding his car together were the scratches.

Time to be a sit-down comedian. His anger erupted. He blurted out, 'That's it! I am calling the police,' and promptly ran into the nearest shop.

Well, I didn't need that and neither did the police, or him, so I followed him in. I thought he must have been having a really bad day. And it could get worse.

I could have thought, 'How dare he treat me like that,' and retorted in a similar tone to create more conflict. That would have made matters worse and we could have come to blows; in which case, I would have needed an ambulance. Physician heal thyself doesn't cut the mustard when you are hurt or unconscious.

Instead of feeling angry, I began to feel sorry for the guy. The fear of getting hurt wasn't my only reason for feeling sorry for him. If you step outside your natural desire to react and can control your internal emotion, you can more easily analyse other people's anger. I felt he must have something really bad happening in his life or day to overreact in such a way.

He needed sympathy, calming down and a solution for his problem. I didn't need the hassle of dealing with the police paperwork and further disruption to my day. As I was insured I wrote down my name and insurer and said I would happily pay for any damage. I also said that I was sorry that I had rear-ended him and didn't mean to ruin his day. I was from out of town and was looking at a map and my foot had slipped. I apologised again and said I would make good any damage. I ventured to suggest that he must be really under stress to react like that and that I didn't want to make it worse.

I wasn't prepared for his reaction. He nearly burst into tears and started to tell me how he'd had a bad day, that he'd been rear-ended a few years ago and had a painful neck and chronic headaches ever since. He then apologised to me for overreacting. We swapped phone numbers and sure enough he phoned to say that a claim wasn't coming as he had calmed down.

Thus I began to learn that, even in heavily emotionally charged situations, I could completely change the shape of my world by using Emotional Algebra.

Once you understand and manage your own internal conflict, you can better manage external conflicts.

Chapter 12

Sometimes not getting what you want is a good thing

Whatever has happened in the past exists only in your memory. Whatever will happen in the future exists only in your imagination. The only thing that is real is what is happening right now — you reading this book.

As mentioned in part two, you have many choices to make in life. Remember each situation you face can generate seven different thoughts with seven different actions; each one of those can create another seven thoughts and actions. If you face ten different situations in one day, that gives you 282 million choices.

This book is about making the right choice. It is also about making the best of the situation you are in, regardless of choice. If you choose the wrong path, you can still choose to enjoy that path while you figure out whether to improve it or to choose another.

Recently I was talking to a client who organises her business life in six-minute blocks to create efficiency. On deeper questioning I found she spent one minute stressing about what she did in the last six-minute block and two minutes being stressed about what was coming up later in the day or week. This was a 50 percent reduction in productivity and a waste of time.

You can't change the past, so why worry about it? The future holds so many variables and unknown outcomes that you may be getting stressed about something that might not happen. I say if one door closes, a thousand other ones open. Surely that is what makes life so exciting.

Those of you who have done a lot of travelling will have learnt not to get stressed if things don't go your way; that's if you want to enjoy the trip.

I remember one of the most relaxing moments of my life while travelling. I was trying to hitchhike from Sydney to Melbourne around the coastal route. I had been standing for a few hours at an intersection of highways with no luck. I noticed most of the cars were turning inland towards the Snowy Mountains. I checked my map and found I could get to Melbourne that way, which I hadn't thought of.

I crossed the road and immediately got picked up. My life changed. I met a new good friend a day later on the inland route, fell in love with her and ended up living in Canada with her for a few months. The point is that I didn't get stressed because one option wasn't working. I enjoyed my few hours at that spot, I took some great photos, relaxed and was happy in the moment.

You may argue that I wasn't in a hurry, stuck in traffic or

late for a meeting. The same principle still applies. What is the point of getting stressed? If you are stuck in a big traffic jam, stressing out will only make it worse. Throwing a tantrum if you are rejected or disappointed won't help matters either. Your blood pressure will increase and you are more likely to make bad decisions in the heat of the moment. I am sure Healthy Thinking will lower your blood pressure. It has mine.

The way to relax is to change your thinking. Worrying about being late won't free up the traffic. You are better to enjoy the music and the view and relax. Use the few extra minutes to think about what you need to do to prepare mentally for the day. Think of how lucky you are. If you feel unlucky, think about how you might avoid this traffic in the future: change your route, leave earlier, leave later, catch the train, change your job and move to the country. Look at the clouds. Enjoy being alive. There is plenty of time to be in a hurry when you are dead.

I remember recently being late for work in a busy rural general practice. I was driving along Surf Highway 45 behind a stock truck. Effluent was spilling from the truck and splashing onto my car. I had about 20 kilometres to go and I knew I would be late for the clinic. I felt irritated that my car was being splashed with cow manure and pulled up close to pass.

Checking myself, I thought, 'Why risk overtaking on this stretch of road?' A better strategy was to take my foot completely off the accelerator, which I did. The truck carried on and the splashing stopped. Around the corner came a speeding milk tanker towards me. If I had overtaken I may have been collected and killed by this thing. The sun came out and shone on the snow-capped volcano. What a view!

Around the next corner the stock truck was indicating and pulled off the road to go onto a farm.

Sometimes slowing down is more productive than speeding up. We seem to live life with our foot flat to the floor and on a fixed track to the end. This isn't exciting or healthy. Sometimes not getting what you want is a good thing.

I describe stress as being the gap between expectation and delivery. If I expect someone to behave in a way and they don't, I could find it stressful. If I expect to win a comedy competition and I don't, I could be disappointed or stressed. If I miss a plane and have to catch another one, I could rant and rave and get upset but it isn't going to bring the plane back. I might meet an important client on the later plane or avoid an accident by not rushing for the first one.

Stress is born, lives and dies
between our ears.

Chapter 13

New thoughts, new adventures

The most enjoyable and rewarding venture I have done thus far is to transform myself into The Attitude Doctor. Once I had learnt how to do Healthy Thinking and Emotional Algebra, my emotions were under control. I set about having some fun exploring. Using my new-found ability to control my thoughts and emotions I had a good basis to again attack life. I also set out to teach others what I had discovered.

This chapter is more about how you can have fun and enjoy the moment than anything else. It shows you how freeing your mind and behaviour from unhealthy emotions can create space for greater enjoyment of the moment.

We change our clothes every day so why not our attitude? Our internal approach to life and situations can be used like the television channel remote control. The more channels you have, the better you are. I am amazed at how many people persist with the same attitude despite it not working for years. It is far easier to change your attitude than the situation.

One of my other keys to success is the ability to seize opportunity and be impulsive. This is a key area for most entrepreneurs. The two best tools I use are the telephone and the ability to say yes. For some years now I have been the doctor for the Fijian rugby team and have toured Italy and France with the side.

I had been the doctor for the local national provincial championship rugby team, Taranaki. We had won the Ranfurly Shield off Auckland, and I had enjoyed being part of that. So one day, I rang Fiji and talked to the coach of the Fijian rugby team, at that time a man called Brad Johnstone.

After explaining who I was and establishing that I had the necessary skills and qualifications, I asked him if he needed a doctor for the Fijian national rugby team.

After he said yes, I asked him when the next game was. 'Saturday,' he replied, which was three days away.

'Who are you playing?' I enquired.

'Japan,' came the reply.

'I'll be there,' I said and turned up with my medical bag.

That simple phone call began what has been a close association with Fiji, a beautiful Pacific tropical island nation that is becoming my second home. The opportunities that have opened up by being the doctor in a religious country for which rugby is almost a religion are huge and, although I could not earn a living from it, there is a lot more to life than money.

Not only have I met many good people, I have also had enormous fun. Like the time the manager of the Fijian team could not go to the official team dinner the night before Fiji played France in a test match in France. I offered to go and was the official Fiji representative at one of the best dinners of my life. The food, the wine and the company was outstanding, and I did my best by singing Fijian songs and telling stories about Fiji. I have made many friends and have many more to come, I'm sure.

An affinity for islands seems to be part of my make-up. A group of islands some 850 kilometres off the east coast of New Zealand, called the Chatham Islands, is located at 45 degrees south, on the way to South America in the Roaring Forties of the South Pacific Ocean. The islands have a population of 650 people, a small hospital, lobster, oysters, scallops, wild pigs, surf, and endless large fish including a population of great white sharks. Every now and then the white pointers savage the local paua divers. The islands had been the base of South Pacific whaling and a penal colony, and had an impressive history with warring of local indigenous tribes, the Maori and Moriori, my children's ancestors.

Working there had always appealed to me, as I had always wanted to visit the islands. Once again unhealthy thinking nearly stopped me: I didn't think I had had enough experience delivering babies. A brother of a friend owned the airline that flies the Chathams. His son was unwell and my friend asked if I could phone him to help. I offered to help and was surprised by his offer of a return trip to the island. I figured there was no time to waste so said, 'What are you doing this weekend?'

'Nothing,' came the stunned reply, so I packed a bag and headed off. At the time I had a broken leg in a plaster cast, having fractured it jumping on to my yacht some weeks before. Changing to a fibreglass cast, I headed off to the remote and rugged Chathams. The cast didn't involve the ankle so I was able to drive a car while on the island.

Once on the ground I was loaned a pick-up truck and I set off to explore the coastline for potential surf and fishing spots: Healthy Thinking and healthy lifestyle. I arrived at a small settlement called Port Hutt that must be one of the remotest communities on the planet: a dot in the middle of the great Southern Ocean.

I saw a fishing boat tied to the wharf and wandered down to it, limping with my broken leg.

'You must be the insurance assessor,' the fisherman said.

'No!' I replied.

The bush telegraph had been working and new arrivals on the island were known about and expected. Within a minute I was offered a lift on the boat to check the nets.

The surf was small but world class and I was excited. I asked the fisherman why no one surfed. He laughed and began to pull in the first net, which was in between the land and the surf break. A very large blue moki fish came up in the net with a very large hole in it obviously made by an even larger shark. White pointers up to 20 feet long had been seen in close — *very* large sharks.

We pulled in several hundred kilos of prime fish in a

short space of time and headed back to the only building on the wharf, a fish factory. I was given a tour of the factory and, as a gift, a few kilos of the freshest deep-water alfonsino and bluenose fish you could possibly imagine.

It struck me how one of the remotest, most isolated places in the world could be one of the most friendly. I had lived in San Francisco for four months some years earlier while working at a hospital there. One of the most populated places in the world was, for me, one of the loneliest.

Each night I would go to my apartment in San Francisco, unlock my three safety locks and enter. Occasionally I would see other people in the same apartment block and say hello. They would look scared and try to undo their four safety locks even quicker to enter their fortress — or cell, as it seemed to me.

On the Chathams no one locks their house or car as there are few ways to get off the island: none by car! Don't get me wrong, San Francisco is a great place and I enjoyed it too but any big city can be very lonely if you don't know anyone.

With my large bag of fish, I called in to see my new friend who had lent me the pick-up truck.

I then headed off to my accommodation at the only hotel on the island. After I watched a game of rugby on the big screen I was invited to a twenty-first birthday party. I said yes and found myself travelling 25 kilometres to a remote part of the island where a party was in full swing.

I had not realised it was so far away so had to wait until 3 a.m. for a lift home.

At the party I had said I was keen to go fishing at some stage. And at 6 a.m. the same morning there was a loud banging on the door of my room and I wished I had the three safety locks of San Francisco.

'Do you want to go fishing or not?' a booming voice yelled. The bush telegraph was working again.

'Yes,' I said without hesitation.

In the dark we drove to another wharf and then rowed a small dinghy out to a fishing boat. It was winter and cold. A big four-metre swell was running. The wind was up a bit but I had been to sea a few times and wasn't fazed.

'I have never been seasick yet,' I said to the skipper.

'You've obviously never been in a big enough sea or a small enough boat,' came the reply.

Well, this was a big sea and a small boat and my leg was in plaster. I soon found out that the deckhand was sick and I wasn't there for a scenic tour. I was there to work. My job was to break the frozen abalone offal and put it into plastic containers. These went into the ten pots we lowered to catch huge blue cod. They were as big as my lower leg without the plaster. In a process known as codding, we would circle around the pots until we had caught literally a ton of fish.

It was cold. My hands were cold from the weather let alone the frozen abalone and I wished I hadn't said yes to the copious amounts of rum offered at the party the night before. However, the albatrosses, the sheer cliffs, the steel- green sea and the clunk of the diesel motor made it all worthwhile. It was hard to sit on the rolling deck with one leg straight and bleed the fish at the same time but I managed. In fact, I loved it.

As the sun set, we dropped anchor after a full day's codding. We had set a few lobster pots too, and picked up a nice feed of lobster. I was dropped off at the hotel to find it dark and deserted with a note on my door.

> Dear Tom. We have gone to the other side of the island. Help yourself. See you in the morning.

The hotel was open, so I uncorked a cold bottle of Chardonnay, lit the fire and started cooking lobster. The next morning I flew home but had been offered a job running the island's hospital over the summer. I quickly accepted.

I returned to the Chatham Islands some months later and had two weeks there on my own before my family arrived. In that time I surfed, dived, fished, doctored and had the time of my life. I lived in the moment. I have a photo of my children rushing off the plane to meet me. A picture tells a thousand words of the happiness of a new adventure and seeing Dad.

We spent another month on the islands and had the most magical time. Whatever the future may hold, the time my family and I spent on the Chathams was very special. We made lots of friends, I surfed despite the fear of great white sharks and did house calls to other remote islands on lobster boats. We swam and fished and played until the sun set. We had an endless summer. I dived for abalone and lobster, found fossils and sharks' teeth, and my children saw albatrosses and the tree carvings of their ancestors. They roamed with complete freedom. A better time or place would be hard to imagine. Healthy Thinking had got me there. If it wasn't for that, who knows …

Two years after being divorced I thought it might be time to try a new relationship. I had taken the time to sort myself out and was confident that I could cope with a female friend. As I live in a very small farming community, I knew the chances of meeting a Julia Roberts look-alike locally were slim. I also didn't want to form new relationships too close to home in case my children found out and were affected by it.

Having started an Internet company, I thought I would try Internet dating. It made sense to me as, when my kids were tucked up asleep at night, I could tap away at the keys. I chose a reputable site, posted my photo and waited. I also clicked on a few profiles including a Spanish princess who, as coincidence would have it, looked like Julia Roberts.

She and I began to communicate. After six months of emails and many phone calls I was ready to take the plunge. I booked a yacht, also on the Internet, and decided to circumnavigate the island of Mallorca with her; to test the waters so to speak.

It was a cold winter's day in New Zealand and one of my good friends was having a birthday party. There was a gathering of friends before the taxi arrived to take me to the airport to leave for Spain. You can imagine I was subjected to much banter and confidence-undermining.

'How do you know she isn't a man?'

'If she is, it will be a very short sailing trip,' I replied.

'How do you know she hasn't just cut and pasted her photo out of a fashion magazine?' another one chuckled.

'I don't; that's why I am going to find out,' I retorted.

They were all laughing as the taxi pulled up to take me across the world from New Zealand to Barcelona. I had been fortunate enough to be upgraded to first class the whole way so I said, 'I'll tell you what. You guys all stay here in the rain and laugh at me. I'll fly first class to the warmth of Spain and go sailing for a week with a Spanish princess!'

They all looked bemused and realised the truth of the statement. Better to go and follow the dream.

Two weeks later I was sailing across a pristine bay. It was warm. The sun was just coming up and my authentic Spanish friend was still asleep. She hadn't cut and pasted anything and we got on very well.

Suddenly I thought of my children and felt guilty. I was thinking I was being a bad parent by enjoying myself sailing. Time for some Emotional Algebra.

Was it true that I was being a bad parent?

No!

Was the thought helping me achieve my goal?
No!

Would the thought make any difference to my children?
No!

I changed my thought to:

> In two days I will be home in the New Zealand winter again. The house will be untidy. I will have chores to do on my own, lunches to cut and washing to do. My children are expecting me home with presents and a smile. Me feeling guilty is not going to make any difference to their day today. They won't know and it will just spoil my trip. I could choose to feel bad but it won't make them feel better. I am allowed a holiday. My parents went away occasionally when I was young. If I had still been married I would have wanted to take my wife sailing by ourselves anyway. In fact, we had gone sailing without the children before we got divorced.

There is a difference between guilt and conscience but in my view guilt, like jealousy, is a complete waste of time. If your partner chooses to be with someone else it is for a good reason. Better to accept the fact and get on with life.

By changing my thoughts in such ways, I changed how I felt. I looked at the castles on the hills and the small fishing boat at starboard and felt alive. My frown was replaced with a smile and I thoroughly enjoyed the day. My children's day was unaffected.

I was glad to be home when I did arrive, having tested the Spanish waters but found I wasn't ready for commitment at that time.

All too often I see people substituting one unhealthy relationship for another because they fear being on their own. You must first learn to like yourself and your own company. You should be optimistic that you will find someone else. Sometimes that person needs to be you.

It is easy to think of ten things to make yourself miserable but sometimes harder to think of ten things to make yourself happy. Apparently optimistic people live 19 percent longer than pessimistic people. It's good for your health to be optimistic. The more you practise, the better you get at it. One of the major things I see that people take for granted is their health.

I often have had to tell people they don't have long to live. To see someone change their attitude in the last days of their life is humbling but also a reminder that we shouldn't just change our attitude because our number is up. It's a lot more fun to change attitude because you want to rather than because you have to. The attitude tool that I have developed shows people how they are thinking and how it affects their emotions, behaviour and productivity. Emotional Algebra is the tool to recognise thoughts and change them to produce a more productive and happy life as a result. If you feel you need a refresher read part two again.

Be impulsive.

Do things you have always wanted to do.

Take some risks and have fun at the same time.

Another example of changing your attitude to deal with the situation rather than changing the situation happened on that recent tour to Fiji with Mike King I mentioned earlier.

I had to fly economy class. I normally travel business class, being a big, tall guy. I dread what is dubbed cattle class as it's cramped. I have become used to the luxury of plenty of room, and good food and wine. However business class was full so I lumbered down the aisle like a bear with a sore paw looking for my window exit row seat, which is normally roomy. Not in a 767. The bulkhead meant my knees were hard against the wall.

To make matters worse, the exit window was so small I was sure I couldn't get through it if there was an emergency and the guy next to me was about 19 years old and wanted to know everything. Not only that but the movie screen was about 2 feet (60 centimetres) in front of my face but 3 feet (1 metre) to the left, which didn't make for good viewing. Why didn't I book earlier?

These thoughts set off the warning bells of unhealthy thinking. Being disappointed wasn't going to move the bulkhead or reduce the flight time. I could choose to sit there for three hours like a spoilt brat wishing I was

somewhere else or I could choose a different attitude and have some fun.

So I took off the headset and starting talking and listening. The whole attitude was different down the back. They were there to party. The call button was pressed and my cheeky neighbour asked the steward for more drinks for both of us. It was different to what I remembered. The laconic boredom and stuffiness of inhibited business class was replaced by the first-time enthusiasm of new travellers on a new adventure.

Sure it was cramped and the food selection wasn't as good but people were having fun and weren't afraid to laugh. I was glad I joined in and chose to change my attitude and internal clock. I might otherwise have missed a great party.

I'm not putting down those in business class but it isn't cool to whoop and cheer up the front. Maybe I'll try it next time. Maybe it is but no one wants to! So if you see some bald-headed giant in business class trying to inject some enthusiasm, chances are it's me!

My Attitude Doctor work (www.theattitudedoctor.com) is going very well. I am heavily booked as a motivational speaker, including being confirmed as the keynote speaker for a nationwide speaking tour of 12 cities. Microsoft, Hewlett Packard and Telecom, working through the Chamber of Commerce, run this tour conjointly. This for me is a great opportunity to eliminate a lot of unhealthy thinking; to help many businesses get ahead. In a short space of time, through a worthwhile forum called Business Club (www.businessclub.co.nz) I have spoken to many individuals and corporates, and my workshops on stress, emotions and success are in great demand. The power of Healthy Thinking is stunning.

To be able to speak about what I passionately believe in is a dream coming true. Whoever said that all good things come to those who stand and wait obviously wasn't in business. I say all great things come to those who get out and hustle!

I certainly have been doing that. I have been doing Healthy Thinking talks and workshops at every opportunity and making minor attitude adjustments about everyone I meet if needed. Getting to meetings and meeting people is part of *making a difference.*

Over recent months I have spoken to countless individuals and groups about the power of Healthy Thinking. It has taken me to many places I never dreamt of getting to. Many people have gained benefit and encouraged me to write this book. Healthy Thinking is simple but very effective.

The power of Healthy Thinking
is stunning.

It will take you places you
never dreamed possible.

My goal is to be a successful motivational speaker and comedian. My behaviour needs to reflect that. My attitude needs to be one of accepting criticism. When people tell me what I am doing wrong, I take it as a chance to improve. I don t play the blame game or denial game. Getting feedback is important in all walks of life. Hecklers while you are on stage give a very immediate type of feedback, and that is a great way to hone your skills.

Part four

Success Behaviours

Chapter 14

What is success?

You have discovered Healthy Thinking, used Emotional Algebra and selected your attitude. Now you are sufficiently in control of your life to seek out success — living out your dreams and goals. Don't leave your dreams as tempting but unachieved hallucinations. Act to bring them about through the use of Healthy Thinking, Emotional Algebra and success-oriented behaviour.

Success is relative. The more successful you are, the more relatives you have got.

We can define success in many ways. I use the ten Cs to success outlined in the next chapter when teaching groups how I have built so many businesses and opportunities in my life. This is my prescription. It works and continues to work for me and others. But you may want to write your own: whatever works for you to achieve your goals.

People often think:

> I will be happy when I buy a new car, a new luxury yacht or a new sweater.

You can be happy while you are heading towards a goal. You can get satisfaction and enjoyment from reaching the goal. Sometimes the fun is in the ride. Don't forget that.

A common indicator of success is money. It is a great thing but having it brings its own set of problems, just like not having it.

Having good friends is another key indicator. I know some very rich people who complain they don't have many friends. They say, rather than friends, they have 'rent-a-crowd', people who associate with them because of the money and lifestyle. They are almost paranoid, feeling that they can't trust anyone's motives. They aren't sure if their 'friends' like them or their money.

If you have no money you don't have this problem. You can be secure that your friends are there because they like you.

One of my key indicators of success is how much better you can make people's lives. Every day when I drop my children off at school I say, 'Have I told you kids how much I love you today?'

'More than anything in the whole universe!' comes the reply.

'That's right, now remember to smile and be nice to everyone you meet.'

'Okay, Dad. We love you!' and they skip into school.

Now don't get me wrong. There are days when my kids don't do as they are told; when we are late and flustered. One morning before school, my daughter was trying to ice a cake she'd made. She didn't listen and spilt icing sugar all over the floor as we were leaving. I lost my cool for a few seconds.

Thankfully, Emotional Algebra turned the situation around. I recovered my composure and apologised, and we parted friends. I watched the kids again skip into school. We are developing some attitudes and strategies to avoid a repeat performance. If my mother had spilt the icing sugar I wouldn't have stressed, probably because I knew she could clean it up.

My point is, again, who needs enemies? Being nice to people brings internal and external rewards. On my way back from Fiji recently I met a friend at the airport. She told me how a waitress at a restaurant had asked her to bring shoes for her children on her next visit to Fiji. My friend was taken aback and felt uncomfortable that a person would ask for something in this way. She wasn't going to respond as requested. I told her she should. It would make a little girl and her mother very happy, which is success itself. It may get her exceptional service and table priority at her next visit to the restaurant and she will feel good having given shoes to someone who needs them.

I have found that you always receive back at least twice as much as you give. It's a multiplication thing. Remember though, two times zero is zero.

Measuring success is not always possible in tangible terms. Success can be how you feel inside and being content with the moment. Remember it will never come again. One day my little girl will have her own house. The icing sugar she spilt on our floor got wiped away. I hope she remembers that I was sorry I got cross, that we kissed and made up and that she still skipped into school feeling special.

A few years ago at the end of the *60 Minutes* documentary on my exploits I was asked, 'What is your next goal?'

'To coach the Coastal sixth grade rugby team,' was my answer.

Death is only a heartbeat away. I have stared it in the face many times, from surviving a tidal wave of water to surviving a tidal wave of depression plus a few near misses in between.

Remember that what has happened in the past is only in your memory and what is happening in the future is only in your imagination. Enjoy where you are now because it is real. Do not wish your life away. Enjoy the journey, go with the flow and make the most of each opportunity. Remember the choices you have and make life exciting.

Smile and laugh, and you will feel better. So will the people around you. Laughter is a great medicine. It is infectious and has even been shown to boost our immune response.

Learn to stop and listen. We are all rushing somewhere. Listen to yourself, to those around you and your children. Listen to the wind, the rustle of leaves, the sound of traffic and the sound of your heart. Enjoy each moment. Stay healthy in yourself by Healthy Thinking.

Chapter 15

The ten Cs to success

You can apply these ten Cs to success to any goal: from starting a business, choosing a partner, dealing with elderly parents or young children, to getting an Olympic gold medal. They could be called the ten commandments of modern-day success. One of the most popular workshops I do involves these ten Cs. They are a formula for achieving success, either in business or personal life.

Recently I gave a seminar and didn't mention the ten Cs. I was impressed when one member of the audience came up to the whiteboard and wrote, in the correct order, my ten Cs. She told the group how she had been using them, and how powerful they had been as a set of guidelines. She had attended a previous seminar and had remembered them. I said, with a wink, that I was pleased she had found them useful but there were actually 11 Cs — the last one being copyright!

The ten Cs to success are listed in the box on the following page.

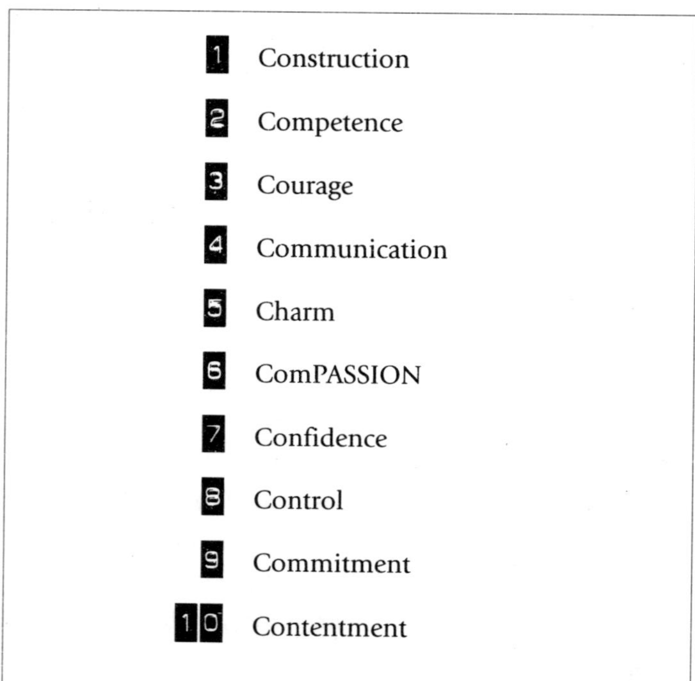

1. Construction
2. Competence
3. Courage
4. Communication
5. Charm
6. ComPASSION
7. Confidence
8. Control
9. Commitment
10. Contentment

I will discuss each one briefly.

1 Construction

You need to construct a plan — a vision of where you want to go and how to get there. Writing a business plan or personal goals is the first step. As I showed earlier, you need to select the attitudes to get you to where you want to go.

If you aren't getting what you want, change your attitude and that will get you to where you want to be. To help you, there is plenty of software available for writing business plans as well as books in the library or business mentors and coaches.

One of the best lessons I learnt was when I entered my first business award. Having my business plan in my head wasn't good enough for the judges. Formalising it into a document helped the strategy and direction. It also enabled other people involved in the organisation to know where I was going. It is a prerequisite if you are looking for finance or venture capital.

2 Competence

I doubt I will ever be successful as a painter or opera singer. I am incompetent at both. While training and development may help, you need to have some talent in the area in which you want to be successful.

This may sound obvious, but in my business mentoring I have seen some people who have few skills in an area wanting to be successful in that area. While I believe you can achieve anything you set your mind to, it is a lot harder work if you aren't basically competent in that area. In most instances, the path of least resistance is easier to follow.

When composing a plan for a new business, write down what you are good at and what you enjoy doing. Often this process will help you identify a niche in the market you can create or occupy. If you are a chef and like learning French, you may want to travel to France and specialise in French cuisine. If you like motorbikes and are a teacher, maybe you could start a school that teaches people to ride motorbikes. All occupations have a barrier to entry. That barrier is usually strongly based around competence, training and qualifications.

If you have grown tired of working in your core area of expertise, it may be best to try new niches within its boundaries or that use strong skills you have learnt from your involvement in that area of endeavour. Success will come more quickly if you avoid trying to reinvent yourself from scratch.

Quality, too, is necessary for success and is harder to achieve when competence is lacking. If you lack some competency, train yourself or find competent staff to help you to achieve it.

3 Courage

Courage is hugely important. Sometimes you need to take risks. You may have to change direction, think outside the square and try new ways of doing old things. This may make people who are used to the same diet of behaviour uncomfortable. It may make you uncomfortable. If you believe in the direction you are headed and the result you are seeking, then you need to have the courage of that conviction.

A strong sense of self-belief and courage is essential when times are tough. It took courage to do many of the things I have done. Writing this book and admitting I have suffered depression took courage. When I started the book

I had no intention of doing so. The more I wrote, the more I knew I had to. Overcoming depression takes courage. Hiding it makes it worse.

When I did my stand-up comedy gig in front of 850 people, it was the courage to do it that impressed people as much as the jokes. Courage is also important in being honest and being able to laugh at yourself. It's also essential for admitting when you are wrong or have made a mistake.

4 Communication

Having been in charge of a busy medical clinic for a number of years I know the importance of communication. Nearly 95 percent of complaints about doctors are due to poor communication, usually involving patients or relatives not understanding what is happening next, what to expect or what to do.

It is well documented that dysfunctional relationships in business or personal life are also usually caused by a lack of effective communication. It is vital that the market, your colleagues and friends understand what is going on.

You saw that unhealthy thinking stems from unhealthy thoughts. These thoughts are often created or fuelled by poor communication and misunderstanding. Choose your words carefully. A communication strategy is a necessary tool for success.

5 Charm

Like it or not, charm is an important ingredient of success. If you want to sell something, charm helps. You may be selling a product, a service, an idea, or yourself. It is important that people like and respect you. Being charming comes easier for some people. For others it takes some work.

Charm is not a quality that will cost you much. A smile, some humour and a genuine interest in other people can make you appear charming. Like all success behaviours, the charm must be appropriate for the situation. Too much charm or charm applied in the wrong measure or situation can backfire.

Your charm must also be backed by honesty and a genuine desire to be nice. It should be a normal part of your total integrity as a personality. Being charming just before you do a bad deal, or stab someone in the back isn't likely to help you achieve success in the long term.

6 ComPASSION

Most human beings are basically the same. We all make mistakes; we all want forgiveness and compassion. As a doctor I have often been confronted with angry people. They may be angry about the situation, their illness, or the system in which they find themselves. Often they are angry with themselves.

I remember one woman being so resentful that she was verbally abusing everyone around her. I simply said, 'It must be awful to have all that resentment inside you.' I was being compassionate, not sarcastic. My comment stopped her in mid-flight. She agreed it was and burst into tears.

Often the unhealthy emotions I mentioned earlier can consume someone. Once the day is filled with unhealthy emotions, the blame game can kick in. Thoughts begin to suggest that it is everyone else making you angry or resentful, not something that is coming from within you. When confronted with such a barrage, instinct tells us to hit back or respond in defence. My view is that compassion is a mighty weapon. If you feel compassion for someone who is in a bad way, it helps you and them.

The PASSION part of the word compassion is all-important. If you don't believe in what you are doing, it will be difficult for others to do so. I am passionate about Healthy Thinking. It is simple but effective. I know it works. I could not write this book, give lectures, seminars or workshops if I didn't believe in it — as I do — passionately.

Sometimes when it is difficult to give a talk or write a paragraph, I remember how passionate I am about it. The spark re-ignites the flame. This applies to any situation.

If you aren't passionate about something or someone try and work out why. Look at your plan. If there is no spark, then it may be time to try something else — another strategy or another attitude. But if the flame is just withering due to lack of fuel, then you know what to do about it.

7 Confidence

Confidence comes from many things: from knowing your subject matter to knowing yourself.

Some people seem born with a large supply. Mostly, people's confidence has good foundation. Without good foundation, confidence can appear as arrogance or stupidity. Confidence needs to be based on fact. Being successful depends on the degree to which your confidence reflects your ability.

Increase your confidence and your ability to perform will also increase. Increase your ability to perform and your confidence will increase. They are directly related.

Stand-up comedy certainly teaches you confidence. If you feel that you can't do it you automatically lack confidence. This creates anxiety in you, impeding your performance, but it is also subtly conveyed to the other person too. This is not good if you require their help.

Train well, be well prepared and then be confident in your ability and know you are. This confidence will show, and bring you greater success.

8 Control

Healthy Thinking is about controlling your thoughts, which control your emotions. Remember you can't have an emotion without having a thought. Recognise the emotion, then control the thought. Change the thought to change the emotion.

Other factors also need control. Growth in start-up

companies is one. You can be a mile wide and very thin. I know from experience. Focus your control on one area. As an entrepreneur I have to control my ideas and sometimes my enthusiasm. It is easy to head off in a multitude of tangential directions, rather than staying with just one direction.

Controlling spending and resource consumption is important. To be honest, control is essential.

9 Commitment

Sometimes the easiest thing to do is to give up. Sometimes you need to. But if you believe in your goal and want to achieve it, you must be committed to it. That means not giving up, even though at times you feel like you want to. You may need to change attitudes and behaviours to get there, but you have to keep going.

Being committed is hard work. I look on a goal like sailing a boat. There are storms along the way, huge waves and difficult winds, gear failure and fog. Each may make you slow down or lose your way. However, sooner or later you will sail into calm weather.

For those of you who have been sailing you will know that feeling, when the sun comes out and you dry all the wet clothing. You pull into a calm bay and reap the rewards. Don't jump off the boat just because the going gets rough. Try to enjoy the whole ride. The good feels so much better when you have had to struggle to get there.

Those of you with children may also know the feeling.

At times you despair and wonder how you could have brought such monsters into this world. At other times you are filled with pride and satisfaction as your children grow and learn to behave themselves appropriately in public.

To reap the rewards you need to be committed. I always had the same view of being married. I expected storms and bad weather, but looked forward to the calm bays and sunshine. Because I believe in commitment, when I said I would be married until death did us part I believed it.

Sailing the family boat is harder by yourself. As the children get older they can help crew and steer the boat too. Sometimes you need help. The calm bays, smiles and love are worth it. The hard work of commitment pays off.

10 Contentment

Contentment is about enjoying the ride. You must be content in the moment, for nothing else exists. If you are always focused on a distant place to which you are heading without also enjoying the ride, you risk missing out on a lot of life.

You need to be riding in a direction, but enjoying what you see and find along the way. It won't come again. You will never be as young and as good-looking as you are now. Make the most of it. Make a list of all the good things you have. Put health at the top of your list if you have it. From experience as a doctor, it is something most of us take for granted.

To be successful you must appreciate what you have,

not be miserable about what you don't have. You have the moment, so make the most of it.

The future is in your imagination.

Who knows what my future will bring? I intend to enjoy it, whatever it is. My long-term goal is to sail around the world.

Next week, my ex-wife and I are taking our children on a skiing holiday; a family holiday. Who knows where the road will take us? Probably to the skifield!

Don't forget to learn and practise
your Emotional Algebra.

Live long and prosper.

Epilogue

This book is a living document. I hope you enjoyed reading it.

It will change in shape and size as time and research goes on. I am interested in feedback as to what you found useful or didn't so I can use it in future editions.

My goal is still to be a successful motivational speaker and comedian. My behaviour needs to reflect that. My attitude needs to be one of accepting criticism. When people tell me what I am doing wrong, I take it as a chance to improve.

I am interested to know if the technique of Healthy Thinking helps you. I am interested to know how I can make it better. If you want to give me feedback on this first edition please do so. You can email me at:

editor@theattitudedoctor.com

I will try to answer all emails and would like, with your agreement, to include suggestions or case histories in subsequent editions of this book, if you show me how Healthy Thinking has changed your life.

Dr Tom Mulholland